Another War, Another Peace

A Novel by

Ronald J. Glasser, M.D.

SUMMIT BOOKS

NEW YORK

This novel is a work of fiction. Names, characters, places and incidents are either the product of the author's imagination or are used fictitiously. Any resemblance to actual events or locales or persons, living or dead, is entirely coincidental.

FIRST EDITION
Library of Congress Cataloging in Publication Data
Glasser, Ronald J.
    Another war, another peace.
    1. Vietnamese Conflict, 1961–1975—
Fiction. I. Title.
PS3557.L35A82   1985   813′.54   85-2646
ISBN 0-671-50767-2

CONTENTS

The 40th   9

The 70th   205

Zama   215

"All I know is that I did all I could."

Trooper, First Air Cavalry
Surgical Ward
U.S. Army Hospital
Camp Zama, Japan

The 40th

Chapter 1

The last bit of darkness clung to the wide surface of the plateau. As the sky brightened, the fog, thinning along the ridge lines, revealed patches of an oceanlike land of shallow basins and barren hills. Far from the horizon, barely touched by the gathering light, a dozen buildings huddled at the edge of a wide depression slowly separated themselves from the morning mists.

It was an unfinished time; a place of shifting forms and changing shapes where shadowy objects appeared one moment only to dissolve away the next, and what was real was only what could be felt. Yet the instant the rim of sun cleared the horizon, the flats burst into light and six hundred square miles of rocky land and dried creek beds, bathed in streaks of orange and pink, froze into stark relief. The buildings, caught in the first rays of the sun, began to glow. The coils of razor wire shimmered with the same strange iridescence; even the walkways and helipad took on a golden hue.

But whatever magic came with the dawn soon faded. Within minutes, the buildings of the 40th had grown worn and shabby again, and the sun, free in the sky, began once more to turn the plateau into a sweltering wasteland.

David, impatient with the corporal, looked again at his watch. Not six-fifteen and already he could taste the salt crusting on his upper lip. The corporal was not even sweating.

"Yes, sir, I can appreciate that, sir." The corporal spoke in a soft Southern drawl. The accent, so unexpectedly American out there in the middle of nowhere, had startled David, but so had everything that had happened since basic, when his orders had been changed to Vietnam. After traveling halfway around the world and then spending three days being shipped back and forth across most of South Vietnam, whatever goodwill remained was quickly evaporating in the heat.

"Look, Corporal," David said, "don't get me wrong. I don't care what you carry. As far as I'm concerned, you can hook a howitzer up to the jeep and tow it along behind us. All I'm saying is that I'm not carrying a weapon."

"Yes, sir," the corporal answered as if David hadn't said a word, "I can understand that, sir, but there ain't gonna be nobody out there who'll know you're a doctor. At twenty meters, there ain't nobody'll know the difference between you and me and any other grunt."

David decided it was hopeless. "Look," he said, "I was told by Major Thorpe that this is a secured area."

"Yes, sir . . . officially."

"Then I see no reason to carry a weapon." He had said the same thing at least three times, but either the corporal was deaf or more stupid than he looked.

"Yes, sir," the corporal went on, "but like I said,

there's just gonna be the two of us out there. Don't get me wrong, sir. I ain't saying it's the Ashow Valley around here, but it ain't the States either."

David looked at his watch again. "I thought we were supposed to be out of here by now."

For a moment, David thought he'd have to give his first order, but after a few seconds the corporal, to David's relief, nodded in agreement and gave the cloudless sky an appraising look. "Gonna be another scorcher."

David sighed. "Then maybe we'd better get going before it gets much hotter."

"Yes, sir." The corporal picked up his rifle and walked over to the jeep. He put the rifle next to him on the seat. David, climbing in, expected the argument to continue, but instead the corporal, acting as if nothing had happened, pointed to the backseat. "I've taken an extra brace of canteens. This here heat takes some gettin' used to."

David nodded.

They drove down the main street of the 40th past the Quonset huts and sandbagged buildings and on toward the gate. Groups of soldiers, some with weapons, a few in flak vests, looked up as they passed. There were no guards. They drove through the opening in the fence, past the coils of razor wire and claymore mines, out into the flats that surrounded the base.

David tried to relax, but the heat was unbearable and within minutes he was drenched with sweat.

Lieutenant Colonel Cramer, the hospital commander at the 40th, had apologized for sending him out his first day, but as the colonel explained, the duty was routine and the military command in Saigon had put a new priority on the medical civilian assistant programs, particularly in recently secured areas.

"We're right here," Cramer said, taking him to the topographical map tacked to the back of the dispensary door. "This whole area around the 40th was the bottom of a huge lake that was supposed to have drained into the South China Sea a couple of million years ago to form the Gulf of Tonkin. In the summer it's rocky paddy fields and dry creeks. In the rainy season it's mud. There are a couple of hilly areas north and east of here. The northern ones merge into the mountains of the central highlands. The area military command has set up as our med caps, which is what we call the medical assistant program, begins here"—he pointed to the area directly below the 40th—"and moves up through an arc to the west of us, ending directly north of the fortieth in those hills. The program calls for going out every other day, completing one full swing through our assigned area every three weeks and then starting over again. It's mostly handing out pills. Corporal Griffen will be your driver. He's been part of the program since it started. He's a good soldier. I would have liked to have assigned you a medic but we're short of corpsmen. If there's anything you think you need, let me know. It may take awhile for big items but the small ones we can get for you right away. It's all pretty routine," Cramer added.

Sergeant Bradford, the NCO in charge of the motor pool, was more specific about the missions, if less supportive. After breakfast, the two of them walked out to the motor pool together.

"We've just started these medical civilian aid missions," he said as they walked along, "but the rest of Nam has had 'em for a while. This here area around the 40th was a free-fire zone until three months ago—got hit hard, but there ain't been no trouble since then. Captain Morril did this before you and picked Corporal Griffen to be his driver. Major Thorpe agreed with Colonel Cramer that it was best to keep Griffen on with you. He was a ranger with the 9th before he got reassigned up here. Hard-core but"—the sergeant hesitated—"he'll listen, and," he went on, becoming quite serious, as if it were important for David to know, "he ain't on no drugs."

A quarter-mile east of the 40th they turned off onto a narrow dirt road that wove its way through miles of rock-hard paddies. There was no breeze. The still air concentrated the heat, keeping it close to the ground so that driving across the plateau was like moving through a great blast furnace. The sunlight worked its way around the edges of David's sunglasses, forcing him to squint whenever he looked toward the sun, at the same time giving everything around him a strange blinding clarity. Rocks and shrubs that in the States would have blended with their surroundings stood out one from the other, while the shadows crisscrossing the shimmering landscape began and ended with such geometrical precision that David found he'd lost all sense of distance. There was nothing familiar about the plateau, nothing comforting.

"How do you pronounce the name of the village?" he asked to break the silence.

" 'Doc Tai,' sir." The corporal spoke without taking his eyes off the road. "The gooks pronounce everything with a *Du* in it like *Doc*."

"What's your first name?" David asked.

"Tom."

David sighed, reconciling himself to the silence.

Half an hour later, they entered a series of low-set hills. It grew even hotter. The air became more difficult to breathe. "It must be a hundred and twenty degrees out here," David said, wiping his forehead.

"Yes, sir," the corporal answered. "In the sun anyway. It'll be ten, maybe fifteen degrees cooler when we get into some shade."

"Shade," David said as if the corporal were joking.

Suddenly the jeep jerked to the right. David grabbed the metal windshield to keep from being thrown out. He clenched his teeth in pain.

"Sorry, sir, there was a smooth spot in the road."

"Smooth?" David looked at his hand. There was a three-inch blister etched across his palm.

"The gooks lay out mines. When they put back the dirt, they sometimes do too good a job, leave a little smooth spot."

Clenching his hand, David looked back over his shoulder. Christ, he thought wearily, a year of this, and then he looked again at his burned palm.

David had to force himself to believe that he was really out in the middle of this godforsaken desert, driving around with a Southern cracker who probably hadn't made it through high school, instead of at Walter Reed or Fitzsimmonds. It was not Vietnam, though, that surprised David as much as the fact that he had become part of it.

He'd expected to spend two years in the military; indeed, he had planned for it. David had decided early in medical school that he would be a professor, a doctor's doctor, and the prestigious research fellowship in immunology that he had been awarded as a junior medical student had virtually assured him a future staff position in a university medical school.

The immunology fellowships were scheduled to begin on a certain date. If you could not begin at your assigned time, you would have to wait three or four years for a new position to open. David was scheduled to start his fellowship immediately after completion of his residency in internal medicine; but during his senior year there were rumors of physicians being drafted out of their training programs. Then it happened to someone he knew, a resident who had just started a cardiovascular fellowship. David began to listen more closely to the news and became convinced that despite official pronouncements of success, the war might well interfere with his own plans.

The issue was how to best ensure his future. There was a chance he might be able to start his fellowship on time. There was also the risk of being drafted out of it. David decided something had to be done, and with a little research he discovered that the Army had a deferment plan. The plan allowed physicians to finish their residency and then go into the Army as specialists working at one of the Army's large referral hospitals.

David raised the issue of the deferment plan with Dr. Beeson, the chief of immunology and the professor who had given him the fellowship, and he was surprised that Beeson knew about it. Neither Beeson nor any of his other professors had ever mentioned the war, let alone the possibility that any of their students might be drafted.

"It's not a bad idea," Dr. Beeson had said. "You get to do clinical internal medicine at a first-rate institution. That kind of experience can be of great help in an academic career; and it will help stabilize our program by making sure that you start on time and aren't pulled out unexpectedly." He agreed to change the starting date of David's fellowship to one month after he completed his time in the Army.

David applied for the plan and was accepted. The war *did* go on. By the time David finished his house staff training, there were half a million troops in Vietnam, and the drafting of physicians had become an almost common occurrence.

David received orders during the last month of his residency to report to Fort Sam Houston, Texas, for basic training, and left for Texas the day his house staff training ended. Everything went as planned until the last week of basic. Then the Army announced that all physicians with permanent duty assignments within the continental United States would be reassigned to Southeast Asia unless they voluntarily extended their stateside assignments an extra year. David was as astonished and outraged as the other physicians, who made angry comments about extortion and threatened to call their senators and congressmen, but after the initial shock David realized that for him nothing had really changed. He had his own timetable and was not about to let the Army or anyone else interfere with his future. David was the only physician who refused to extend, and two days later his orders were changed to the 90th Personnel Replacement Center, Saigon.

He was not happy about going to Southeast Asia; his friends and family were not pleased, either, but he'd made his decision and still considered it to be the correct one. Three years in the Army was just too long a time. During basic, a captain in the Rangers giving the lecture on command responsibility had mentioned almost in passing that three doctors had been killed in Vietnam; all of them had been in places they shouldn't have been, doing things they were not authorized to do, taking chances they shouldn't have taken, none of which David intended to do. And, too, though he wouldn't admit it, there was that sense of pride in not having given in either to the Army or to whatever fears he might have unknowingly harbored.

Still, there was a moment at the embarkation center at Oakland when the clerk behind the dispensing counter handed him his flak vest and jungle boots and, seeing the Medical Corps insignia on his collar, hesitated a moment and then, almost as a kind of benediction, whispered, "Good luck."

At the village, Griffen took the jeep off the road up onto a small rise about fifty meters from the first hut and switched off the engine.

"Best to stay out here, sir, and let 'em come to us." He picked up his M-16 and climbed out of the jeep.

David, drained by the heat, looked at the village. Just a dozen thatch-covered huts in a circle. A few scrawny chickens pranced across the dusty ground. Behind the huts the remains of what must once have been a vege-

table garden merged quickly with the rocky countryside. David wiped the sweat out of his eyes and,
gathering his strength, climbed out of the jeep. Griffen
had already started to pile the cartons of medication on
the ground.

"They walk by and pick up the pills?"

"Yes, sir, that's the idea." The corporal continued to
unload the jeep.

David picked up one of the bottles and looked at the
label. "This all we have, Tom? Vitamins, sulfa, iron,
and"—he looked into the next carton—"aspirin?"

"Yes, sir." The corporal picked up one of the canteens, took a sip and handed it to David.

David nodded thanks and took a long drink. The
water was hot and tasted of iodine, but it helped. "Not
very high powered medicine," he said, handing the
canteen back to Tom.

"Well, sir, I guess med command figured these are
the ones that'll travel in the heat." Tom started to put
the bottles on the hood of the jeep.

David began to help, organizing the medications into
rows. While they worked, the villagers began to line
up. Every few moments, Tom would glance up at them.
By the time all the bottles were arranged, a single line
of men and women, infants and children stretched
from the first hut up the rise to within five meters of
the jeep.

These were not the Vietnamese David had seen in
Saigon or at the 90th replacement. What he had considered delicacy in those people had turned to frailty
out here on the flats. These people seemed to have no
weight to them, no substance; they were like creatures

from a lighter planet. David had the uncomfortable feeling that if, indeed, all the fighting was meant to improve these people's lives, the effort had been misguided.

"Looks like everyone decided to come," he said.

"Yes, sir," Tom answered, opening another carton. "All you got to do is motion 'em forward."

David gestured, and the villagers started to file past. Tom replaced the bottles as fast as they were taken.

"They know how to use these?" David asked after a few minutes.

"Use 'em?"

David held up the line and picked up one of the sulfa bottles. "These should be taken every eight hours. Those"—he pointed to the row of iron pills—"three times a day, and the vitamins once a day. They understand that?"

"No, sir, not likely."

"Well, each one of those pills is three hundred and fifty milligrams of iron sulfate. Sixty-five milligrams of pure elemental iron. In the States, they're only used for patients who are severely anemic, and then two, maybe three pills a day for three to six weeks, four pills at the most. If anyone takes a whole bottle of those iron pills or gives five or six at a time to any of these kids, they'll be poisoned."

Tom picked up one of the bottles, looked at the label and then indifferently put it back on the hood. "None of 'em can read, sir."

"Maybe we should have an interpreter with us."

"An interpreter!" Tom was startled. "Look, sir," he said gently, "I don't know what they told you about these civilian aid missions, but they ain't exactly prior-ity stuff. We're lucky they wasted a jeep on us."

David was in no mood to be patronized. "How many of these iron pills have you handed out?" he asked.

"Couple dozen cartons."

"And Captain Morril didn't worry about the dosage?"

"No, sir."

"What kind of physician was he?"

"Kind?"

"What was he?" David asked sharply. "An internist, a GP, what? You must have known what he was."

"I guess he was a surgeon."

David wiped new drops of sweat off his forehead. "That figures. Well, Corporal . . . no matter what else we're going to be doing out here, we're not going to go around poisoning these people. We're going to cut down the number of pills in each bottle."

"They may not like that." David noticed he didn't say *sir*.

"Oh, really."

"They're used to getting whole bottles."

"Corporal," David said, "I'll make a deal with you right now. It'll make both our lives easier. I take care of the medicine, you take care of the driving. Fair enough?"

But the corporal was staring past David so intently that David turned to look himself. Two villagers had stepped onto the top of the rise from the opposite side of the road. When they saw the two Americans, they froze briefly, and then, bowing, quickened their pace as they hurried along to the rear of the line.

"How many pills?" Tom asked.

"What?" David said, confused.

"How many iron pills do you want in each bottle?" Tom was holding the rifle. David hadn't seen him pick it up.

"About a quarter of what's there." David looked back at the two men, both still bowing as they stepped into line. "What just happened?" he asked.

"Nothin', sir. It ain't so good to surprise anyone over here, that's all."

They went to four villages that day. By noon, David was too weary even to talk. He knew he had let himself get out of shape during his internship and residency, but he hadn't thought this much. The six weeks of basic should have helped but they didn't. The muscles in his legs and shoulders were like jelly, and he could hardly breathe. He kept himself going by drinking from the canteens. The water offered little relief from the heat, but he drank it anyway, knowing if he didn't, he'd never make it through the next hour, much less to the end of the day. He didn't notice as he emptied one canteen, then the other, that Tom had stopped his own drinking. They left the last village a little after three. David, exhausted, sank into the seat, ignoring the hot plastic.

For the rest of the trip back, David fought to stay awake. Finally, ahead of them, miles away, they could see the 40th. It lay there, a tiny, square speck almost lost in the reflected glare of the plateau.

"Not much, is it?" But David didn't know whether he thought it or said it.

Half an hour later, they drove back through the main

gate. There were still no guards. The wooden tower near the wire was empty. The base reminded David of some outpost in an old Western movie. He couldn't shake the feeling of amazement at being there. Perhaps he should have extended. Tom drove directly to the motor pool and stopped in front of the office.

"I'll unload the gear," Griffen said, getting out of the jeep.

David didn't offer to help, nor did he go to the hospital; instead, he went straight to the officers' quarters. The old air conditioner over the doorway was rattling away. As soon as he opened the door, the cool air wrapped itself around him. Like a newly pardoned man, he let out a long, relieved sigh, walked over to his cot, lay down, and for the first time since his internship, fell asleep with his clothes on.

Chapter 2

The sunlight coming through the shutters reached the far wall of the barracks. David quickly sat up and then, remembering where he was, relaxed again. Despite the air conditioner, he could feel the layer of warm air rising off the floor. He gave the strips of sunlight a bemused look.

"Well, another scorcher," he mumbled under his breath, mimicking Griffen's drawl. "Damn," he said, realizing he'd fallen asleep in his fatigues. He looked at his watch. Seven o'clock. The barracks was empty. He lay back again on the pillow and stared up at the unpainted rafters. This wasn't going to be as easy as he'd thought, but what was. Anything new was always confusing. There hadn't been one subject, a single course or clinical rotation that hadn't been difficult at first. It took time to know what to do, to get a rhythm going. You just had to stay with it and things would fall into place.

The mess hall was four buildings down from the officers' quarters. There were no curbs or sidewalks, just a wide graded space between two lines of buildings, though it would pass for a street at least, he assumed, till the rainy season.

The officers were all in the officers' mess, a small alcove off the main mess hall. Sergeant Bradford and a couple of other senior NCOs were still in the main area finishing their coffee. David nodded as they gestured hello. He walked over to the food line as Colonel Cramer came out of the officers' area carrying a coffee pitcher.

"Ah," he said cheerfully, "awake." His crew cut and horn-rimmed glasses made him look like a junior executive out of the 1950s.

"Well, up, anyway," David answered.

"A beginning," Cramer said lightly. "Well, get some silverware. They'll fry you eggs . . . how do you like them?"

John Plunkett, the other general medical officer at the 40th, was at the table. A pleasant-looking fellow with an easygoing Midwestern manner, he had been drafted right after his internship and planned, after he went back and finished his training, to open an office in a rural part of Minnesota or Iowa. As far as David could tell from the time they'd spent together the day before, Plunkett bore no ill will toward the Army for having drafted him out of his house staff training. Herb Tyler, the dispensary dermatologist, was sitting across from Plunkett, while Major Thorpe, regular Army and the base commander, sat at the head of the table next to Lieutenant Brown, who doubled as the medical service corps officer, helping out with the hospital, and the officer in charge of the base personnel. It was the same seating arrangement as at lunch the day before.

Cramer made room for David on his right and poured him some coffee.

"How did it go?" Thorpe asked.

"Go?"

"You passed out last night," Plunkett said. "We had a big first-night-back-from-the-boonies party set to go, but you never showed up."

"Show up," David answered good-naturedly. "I was lucky I was able to make it to the barracks." Plunkett laughed.

"They all say that," Cramer said. He handed David the sugar and cream.

"You get used to the heat," Thorpe said.

"Acclimated," Tyler corrected from across the table. "You never get used to it."

Cramer glanced at him, but Tyler had gone back to his eggs. David had met all the doctors and officers the day before. Tyler had been the least friendly. He was a short, round man, no more than five feet four, with large myopic eyes that never seemed to blink. He wore wire-rimmed Army glasses with thick lenses that magnified his stare, giving the impression that he was peering at you rather than just looking at you. The heat at the 40th had worked on him as it had everyone else, but instead of slimming him down it had dried him out, giving him the overall aspect of a dehydrated, if somewhat morose, Buddha.

"First week is always the hardest," Cramer went on. "All the travel, the confusion at the 90th, and," he added, an obvious concession to David's comment, "the heat. Takes awhile for things to settle into place."

"Your driver helpful?" Thorpe asked. The major was

an artillery officer and, according to Sergeant Bradford, a tough but fair commander. The day before, Cramer had mentioned with some pride that this was Thorpe's second tour.

"Helpful but not very talkative." David, not hungry, picked at his eggs.

"He should be helpful," Thorpe said. "He was an LRRP in the Delta—long-range reconnaissance and patrol."

"Ambushed the bastards," Tyler said. "Spread fear and terror among the enemy, things like that."

Thorpe was about to say something but Cramer interrupted. "Anything you need?"

"I'd like to be able to hand out smaller numbers of iron pills. All we have are the three-hundred-fifty-milligram iron sulfate tablets. I don't want to be treating iron poisoning the next time around."

"Good idea. Rick," Cramer said to Lieutenant Brown, "after Captain Seaver's finished breakfast, why don't you take him over to the pharmacy. Lieutenant Brown will get you whatever you want. Anything else?"

"Yeah, an air conditioner for the jeep."

They all laughed.

As he and the lieutenant walked down the street, they kicked up little clouds of fine red dust that hung motionless in the air. There was no breeze, and the sun, as it had the day before, bore down from a cloudless sky. The buildings were all prefabricated plywood with wooden or steel roofs. They were painted Army green and every one was sandbagged up to the windows. A few of the larger Quonset huts had sandbags on their roofs. There were no frills here, no waste. The buildings, like the earth itself, had a grim sparseness. They passed a few enlisted men with M-16s who nodded rather than saluted.

The door to the pharmacy was open. Except for moving the air around, the two large fans inside did little to cool the building. The lieutenant introduced David to the sergeant in charge, Parker.

"Yes, sir," the sergeant answered when David told him what he wanted. "Corporal Griffen was in about just that last night."

"He was?" David said.

"Yes, sir. He explained the problem; said you'd rather lower the dosage of the pills than hand out a smaller number, so I made up twenty-fives instead of the usual three-hundred-fifty-milligram capsules. That's all right, isn't it, sir." It wasn't a question.

"Why sure, yes. That should do it."

"Anything else?" the sergeant asked.

"No . . ." David answered. "Not right now anyway."

He and the lieutenant walked back outside. "Efficient, isn't he?"

"Griffen?"

"Apparently," David answered. "And Captain Morril."

"Oh, Captain Morril liked him. In fact, the rumors were he wouldn't go out on the med caps unless Major Thorpe assigned Corporal Griffen as the driver."

"And Major Thorpe agreed?" David asked. He had learned enough about the Army to know captains didn't tell majors what to do.

The lieutenant hesitated. "Well, Captain Morril had a way of doing the things he wanted."

"What happened to him?"

"The captain went back to the States."

"How long ago was that?"

"Five weeks."

"Who did the med caps till I got here?"

"Did them?" the lieutenant asked. "Why, no one."
David stopped.

"We hadn't been doing it all that long," Brown explained. "Colonel Cramer thought it would be best to wait for you than to start shifting duties around and then have to shift back again."

"And what would have happened if I hadn't been assigned here, if there hadn't been a replacement?"

"Oh," the lieutenant answered noncommittally, "someone would have done it. These civilian programs come right down from military command in Saigon, MACV." It wasn't an answer, but David didn't push it.

David left the lieutenant at the headquarters building and went back to the officers' quarters. He made his bed, organized his gear, and with nothing else to do, went back to the hospital.

Morning sick call was over. Cramer was in his office at the back of the small dispensary, cleaning up some paperwork.

"Get that iron thing settled?" he asked.

"It was settled for me," David said dryly.

The atmosphere of easy goodwill that Cramer tried to exude diminished slightly.

"Oh, it's nothing," David said, seeing Cramer's response. "I guess our Corporal Griffen's just a little more efficient than I expected."

Cramer relaxed and leaned back in his chair. "We

have good people here. Hell, we have good people all over Southeast Asia. In fact," he added with equal seriousness, "all through the military."

Cramer stared at him as if expecting some kind of wisecrack. When David didn't say anything, Cramer regained some of his good humor.

"I don't know what you may have heard about Vietnam," he said, obviously comfortable again, "but I can tell you this—we're winning. Granted, it looks like a lot of little pieces, but the whole thing's controlled, monitored. All you have to do is look at the reports to see how well we're doing. I've been to Saigon. It's amazing how they keep track of everything, fit it all together. MACV has the biggest computers made—IBM and Sperry Rand, dozens of them. I tell you," Cramer said, warming to the topic, "it's amazing. Those generals can find out in an instant exactly what's going on anywhere in Vietnam . . . anywhere! They even know the number of bullets fired per month. The facts put the doomsayers to shame. We'll be out in a year, two at the most. All everyone has to do is his own job. If everyone just does his own job, the whole thing's guaranteed to work."

After lunch, David walked around the base. He hadn't noticed the day before, but half the supply buildings were boarded up. In the middle of the base, encircled by an open cyclone fence, were four concrete huts with steel doors. Open padlocks hung from the doors. On the fence was a hand-painted sign: ARMAMENTS AND AMMUNITION. The motor pool, nothing but an open field next to the munition supply, lined by stacks of fifty-five-gallon drums of gasoline and oil, was empty except for a few jeeps and two armored personnel carriers. Like everything else, the drums and vehicles were covered with a thin layer of red dust. The enlisted men's barracks were behind the motor pool, a group of long, narrow buildings connected by a raised wooden walkway. The sound of Jimi Hendrix drifted across the open ground of the motor pool. In Texas, it had been country music. No Beatles or Brahms in this army. No wonder he didn't know anyone who was in the military.

The helipad lay along the western end of the base, two hundred yards from the motor pool. David walked down the asphalt path past the communications building to the landing area. The path merged with the asphalt apron at the edge of the helipad, the remainder of the landing field nothing more than hard-packed earth. All that separated the 40th from the miles of surrounding countryside was a half-inch of graded dirt.

As he turned away, David noticed on a small platform at the edge of the pad out near the wire a flag drooping in the stagnant air. There was no radar, no wind indicators. So much for the technology and wonders of the modern age, he thought.

Early the next morning the corporal was in the jeep waiting as David emerged from the mess hall. He did not mention the iron pills until they were well out in the flats.

"Yes, sir," Griffen answered. "I was in the pharmacy so I figured I might as well get the iron pill thing out of the way."

"Don't get the wrong idea," David said, making sure he didn't sound too harsh. "I'm not complaining, but I would like to know in advance before you make any changes that affect the medical aspects of these missions."

Tom continued to watch the road.

"It'll make things easier for both of us."

"Yes, sir."

David, not wanting to face a second day of one-word answers, decided to give a little. "You did use your head, though," he admitted. "Cutting down dosages *is* as good as decreasing the number of pills. It's never a good idea," he said with some effort at humor, "to leave patients sicker than you find them."

"Yes, sir," Tom answered flatly, ignoring David's attempt at goodwill, "but I wasn't thinkin' of them gooks."

"Oh."

"I was thinkin' of us. It ain't gonna help any if one of 'em dies and they get it into their heads—or someone puts it there—that we poisoned 'em."

For a moment—but only a moment—David thought he might be joking.

Chapter 3

They went out every other day after that. The searing heat never diminished. There was no place to hide from it. Out in the open, the earth reflected back the heat, mixing with the sunlight so that moving through the flats was like crossing a great blast furnace. The air itself was so suffocating that moving into the shade made almost no difference. Indeed, it was only when they moved back out into the sunlight again that David could sense the little relief the shade had offered. The dust, though, remained the same; all that changed were the lengths of the trips and the sizes of the villages. The villagers, too, remained the same. The old, wrinkled and bent; the women shuffling along; the children staring back with blank expressions.

Tom never talked about the Vietnamese. But he watched them. More than once as they handed out the pills David caught Tom glancing up at a group of villagers who'd stayed out in the fields, or at a man or woman who didn't get into line quickly enough. More than once when David thought they were finished and ready to pack up, Tom would tell him to wait. A few moments later a villager would materialize out of a nearby gulley or appear at the doorway of what David had thought was an empty hut.

Tom remained detached but polite. He'd answer any of David's questions, but the answers were always so to the point that they'd stop any further discussion. He'd make little comments, giving out scraps of information: "The 40th ain't so bad; it can put out a lot of firepower, and with support bases, air strikes are only minutes away." Or "Vitamins ain't no good for nothin'. The gooks like sulfa the best, probably sell 'em on the black market or give 'em to the VC to keep 'em friendly." But he never embellished or pursued an issue, nor did he ever start a conversation. Back at the base, he never sought David out. Despite their long hours together, he acted as if each trip was their first, content, it seemed, as he had been from the beginning, just to drive the jeep and watch the road, hidden behind his sunglasses.

They weren't regular Army issue but the aviator glasses David had seen the pilots wearing when he'd landed at the air base at Tan Son Nhut. Tom never took them off. It didn't matter where they were or what they were doing. They could be in the sunlight or the shade, in the middle of the plateau or at a village, resting or in the jeep. David was sure the glasses with their stylish frames were no more than an adolescent affectation, but after a while they became as annoying as Tom's indifference. David was convinced that anyone, even someone from Georgia, had to know how irritating it was to try to talk to someone constantly wearing dark lenses. If Tom noticed David's growing irritation, he gave no sign of it.

One day they returned to the 40th so late that the

sun, almost at the horizon, crisscrossed the flats with miles of long, thin shadows. The glare of the afternoon was gone and David had taken off his own glasses. He mentioned pointedly that since it was getting darker, Tom might be able to see better if he took off his own glasses.

"Yeah," Tom admitted and then to David's surprise went on as if the comment deserved an explanation. "You might see things in the shade better if you take off your glasses, but then it's hard to pick things out in places still in sunlight or at the edge of the shadows. Once you get acclimated to flight glasses, you can pick up differences in the sun as well as shady areas. You never look directly at an object anyway. You try to look near it—helps pick up subtle changes. If you take your glasses on and off, it's like walking in and out of a tunnel. Takes minutes to acclimate to different lighting; and over here you don't have the time." David wasn't quite sure whether he was being answered or lectured.

Still, David was convinced that Griffen would eventually come around. Clearly he wasn't dumb, and it was obvious that the people at the 40th liked the corporal and, more important, listened to him. The other troopers deferred to him, and on more than one occasion, when Griffen came back from a patrol, David noticed that Thorpe sought him out rather than the sergeant or lieutenant in charge. David expected his own goodwill to wear the corporal down, but by the middle of the second week, like the heat, nothing had changed. Tom retained his distance, so that David began to wonder if Tom understood the advantage of having a captain, much less a doctor, as a friend.

Reluctantly, though, he found himself appreciating Tom's efficiency if not his attitude. The jeep was always ready on time, the medications loaded and the trips worked out in advance so that they never had to double back to get to the second or third village. The numbers and types of pills were exactly what they'd need. One day, after they'd been out for over eight hours, spending a good hour of that sweating and grunting together in the middle of a dried creek bed trying to change a tire whose lug nuts had expanded so much in the heat that they were barely able to get them off, David realized that Tom hadn't once complained; that, indeed, he'd never heard him complain about anything.

David had finally been able to get Tom to stop using *sir* all the time, at least while they were off the base. At the 40th he maintained the formality. "They don't like officers and enlisted personnel to get too friendly," Tom said, and David sensed that Tom believed in the separation.

One day on their way back to the 40th, David deliberately mentioned Captain Morril. He thought he detected a flicker of interest behind Tom's sunglasses.

"Yeah, he was okay," Tom answered and then unexpectedly added, "He was different than other docs."

"Oh? How?" David asked.

Tom turned to look at him. "He liked this shit."

"Anything more specific?" David asked, seeing an opening and determined this time to keep the conversation going.

"He believed in us being here—'better here than the coasts of California' stuff."

"And you don't agree."

Tom shrugged. "It's working."

"Working?"

"We're killin' a lot of people."

"So you don't agree."

"You need a reason for the killin'; I mean sooner or later you need one."

"And California?"

Tom turned and, looking at him, brushed his short, blond hair away from his forehead. "The gooks ain't got any boats."

David laughed. "You know, you do have a point there," he said.

David smiled the rest of the day when he thought of Tom's comment. He mentioned it to Plunkett, who agreed that it had a certain commonsense quality to it. "We got an uneducated army over here, but that doesn't mean they're stupid. Big difference between being dumb and not having gone to college."

It was not only his perception of Tom's abilities that was changing. Over the weeks Tom began to look different to David. Initially, he had considered Tom just a gangly, big-boned kid, but he noticed when Tom was concerned or interested in something, like at the villages when he thought something was wrong, he stood straight as an arrow. He was heavier, too, than he'd seemed at first. He had, David realized as he watched him, more the movements and physique of a gymnast than a basketball player. But it was his eyes that began to hold David's attention. There were those rare times when Tom had his glasses perched on his forehead that David noticed they never stopped moving. David began to realize that there was very little Tom missed, and

what David had thought to be a kind of Southern loose-
ness in Tom turned out to be economy of movement.
In a clean-cut, straightforward way Tom was hand-
some, or would be, David decided, when he was older
and his features sharpened.

As for the rest of the personnel at the 40th, David
found he got along with everyone, even Tyler. In fact,
except for the coolness between Thorpe and Tyler, they
all got along. Tyler's antagonism toward the major was
an embarrassment to everyone, including David, since
Thorpe could have shut Tyler up with one hand tied
behind his back. Tyler's only saving grace was that he
alone among the physicians did any real work.

He spent most of the day in the back of the dispensary mixing up one concoction after another to treat
the endless varieties of skin rashes that flourished in
the heat of Vietnam. David, familiar with the sterility
of university dermatology clinics, viewed the greenish-
brown liquids with misgiving, but soon noticed that
despite the murky colors and obnoxious odors, the lotions and salves did work. While Tyler refused to reveal
what was in his mixtures, he took an alchemist's pride
in their success.

At first, Tyler had put off David's questions about
what he was doing by explaining that it was nothing
but trial-and-error stuff, but when he saw David's appreciation of the results, he began to talk, tentatively at
first, but with conviction, about the antimicrobial qual-
ities of bismuth and arsenic and the absorptive powers
of lotions versus creams.

Tyler was also the only officer who took any interest
in the med caps. He never made a big deal about it, but

David noticed that he'd stop talking or slow down whatever he was doing to listen whenever David mentioned something about Tom or what had happened while they were at one of the villages. It was Tyler who dismissed David's concerns about Tom's behavior with the cryptic "Don't worry. Combat types act that way. If they're quiet, it means they like you."

Chapter 4

What amazed David was how quickly boredom set in. Except for rashes and the occasional cut or bruise, there was nothing much to do at the 40th, but Thorpe made an effort to keep up the morale of the troops, and with some success. He was a big-boned man who demanded discipline, but by his own example. The heat of Nam had worked on him as it had everyone else, so that the skin of his face sagged a bit, making him look older than his thirty-two years. He was always neat and clean shaven, and wore a crew cut that he made a point of keeping perfectly trimmed.

Apparently during his first tour he had been in charge of a battery of four 105-millimeter howitzers. The fire base was hit at dawn, the perimeter overrun in minutes. Thorpe reached his guns before anyone else, cranked down the barrel to zero elevation, quickly loaded the howitzer with shotgun shells and blew away half the attacking force and most of the buildings with the first few rounds. Lieutenant Brown told David that he'd refused a medal because of the three Americans he'd killed in saving the base.

Thorpe fought the boredom. He sent out patrols on a routine basis to keep the personnel fit and, David assumed, alert, and had regular maintenance projects, but he didn't make busywork. If he saw the men sitting around, he let them sit. David found that despite Thorpe's refusal to admit that anything the Army did might be wrong or, at best, ill conceived, he liked him, though he agreed with Plunkett that you wouldn't be inclined to invite him to a formal dinner party.

Plunkett liked not having anything to do. He had his parents send all his medical journals to the 40th and spent two to three hours every afternoon reading them cover to cover, tearing out and filing the articles so that he wouldn't fall behind the physicians in his class who didn't get drafted.

Cramer spent enormous amounts of time at his desk in the dispensary going over rosters and signing requisitions. Every afternoon he walked over to headquarters to talk to Thorpe. What they discussed was a mystery, but Cramer always came back to the hospital with the air of a man who knew his job and did it well.

Brown, with two jobs, seemed to handle the boredom well, though he spent only as much time at the hospital as necessary. David had the sense that he was a bit uncomfortable around doctors, preferring the familiar if more rigid discipline of headquarters.

As for himself, David found that he had begun to look forward to the med caps. Going out to the villages quickly became something to do.

At dinner three weeks to the day after he'd arrived, David said in answer to one of Thorpe's questions that he didn't mind going out into the boonies. There was an embarrassed silence.

"Business is kind of slow around here," David added lightly. No one spoke.

"Well, it wasn't always like this," Plunkett offered, breaking the silence.

"What the good doctor means," Tyler said, "is that there were plans to evacuate this place."

"Herb," Cramer warned.

"There were some actions ten kilometers northwest of here," Thorpe interrupted. It was the first time he or anyone had mentioned actual fighting. "In the hills up near the Kaloo River. The 40th got rocketed a few times, that's all; no real damage."

Tyler reached for the sugar. "And the NVA prisoners?"

"There were always NVA around here," Thorpe said, "and you know it."

"But only as cadre."

"Hell," Thorpe continued, speaking directly to David, "the North Vietnamese have been helping the VC around here ever since the French left."

"These prisoners weren't cadre," Tyler said. "They were from regular North Vietnamese units."

"During the rocketing," Tyler went on, ignoring Thorpe, speaking the word *rocketing* with sarcasm, "they med-evaced NVA in here from units that were supposed to be down in the Delta."

"That was never confirmed," Thorpe said.

"Hold it," Cramer interrupted. "You'll have to excuse Herb," Cramer said, directing his comment to David but speaking to Tyler. "He's never recovered from being transferred away from the glamorous dermatology clinics of Saigon to this humble outpost."

Thorpe began to say something, but Cramer stopped him with one of his rare, cold stares. He could, David had noticed, be quite determined when it came to keeping things moving smoothly.

"The 40th was originally set up about a year ago, as a support base for the Hundred and First Airborne." Cramer stopped before he went on, making sure everyone knew who was now in charge of explanations. "There was a lot of fighting around here then, both VC and NVA"—he looked at Thorpe as if to show his impartiality—"but they cleared out after a couple of weeks. A little later the 40th was upgraded to handle operations into the central highlands and MACV expanded the medical facility into a surgical hospital to support the increased activity."

"The place was hopping," Brown said. Cramer, miffed, glared at him, but Brown continued. "Hell, when I got here there were half a dozen med evac flights a day; ten, twenty wounded coming off each one and all around the clock."

"But that was over three months ago, right, so there's nothing to worry about," Tyler said, speaking to no one in particular.

Cramer ignored him. "The fighting moved off up further north into the mountains, and I Corps and the combat units that had been using the 40th moved out with it; the ARVN moved in and things have been quiet ever since."

"In other words," Thorpe added, still speaking to David, "we beat 'em. Some damn hard battles, too— the 32nd, 33rd and 66th NVA regiments; but we whipped 'em and sent 'em out of those hills with their tails between their legs. We've beat 'em every time we meet 'em."

"Every time you find them would be a more accurate statement."

"Find 'em, beat 'em, the point is we won."

Tyler glanced up from his food. "And what did we get for it?" This time he spoke without sarcasm.

"We have some other things to discuss," Cramer said. But it didn't work. Tyler had gone too far.

"We got the goddamn commies out of here when they wanted to stay."

"You mean, don't you," Tyler answered, "that we sent 'em someplace else." Thorpe flushed angrily.

David wished he hadn't brought up the med caps.

"We won," Thorpe said coldly, "and killed a hell of a lot of them at the same time, and the ones we kill don't go anywhere else."

"Ah," Tyler said, his jowled face brightening, though strangely, David noticed, without any glint of satisfaction. "There we have it, don't we?" Thorpe looked suddenly wary.

"Herb," Cramer said, "what are you getting at?"

"The major knows."

"What I know," Thorpe said angrily, "is that some officers aren't helping."

Tyler put down his fork. "Helping with what?" he asked with a strange, uncharacteristic gentleness. "There are half a million troops over here right now. Need some more fighter bombers or helicopters? How about B-52s? The communists don't even have an air force. Tell me where you want more help and I'll help."

Furious, Thorpe stood up. "If this war's lost," he

fumed, "it'll be because of fools like you." Thorpe almost knocked down two enlisted men as he stormed out of the mess hall.

"A decent man," Tyler said and went back to his meal.

Chapter 5

The next morning David told Tom about the argument. He mentioned it just to make conversation and thought Tom would shrug it off, but he didn't. They were on one of the paved roads so Tom was relaxed, sitting back in his seat. Apparently the VC didn't mine paved roads.

"Captain Tyler's right."

"Tyler?" David said, surprised. He had thought Griffen would have sided with Thorpe.

"All we do is chase 'em somewhere else. When I first got here, there was an effort, at least at division level, to hold ground, but it never worked. There was nothin' to hold. After we took somethin', we'd sit there while the gooks went somewhere else. We'd leave and they'd come back. We'd end up coming back and fighting for the same piece of ground two, three times in a row. Then we went to search-and-destroy operations, swingin' big areas, not holdin' any land, just seein' what we could catch. They were pretty effective, but we stopped 'em. Captain Morril said they got stopped because people at home didn't like to see TV pictures of their hometown boys burnin' down huts of little old Vietnamese women. So now I guess the idea is to go after hard-core units. Try to find 'em and then kill as many of 'em as we can."

"You don't approve."

"Approve." Tom shrugged. "No one asks a rifleman to approve or disapprove things."

"But if you could?"

Tom's expression hardened.

"Well?" David asked.

"We can't kill 'em all. Besides," he went on as if he might have gone too far, "the real fightin' drifts all the time. Makes it tough to keep anythin' goin', to get momentum and keep it up. Things build up quick and go down quick. You can find 'em, but most of the time it slips away from you."

"Like the fighting that went on around here."

"Around here?"

"I've been asking a few questions," David said.

"Yeah, something like that."

"But . . ." David prompted.

Tom looked past him, out across the flats. "When the gooks want something bad enough, they try to get it. If we're there, they'll wait it out if they can—maybe we'll go; but if they need it, they'll come and try to get it."

"You think they'll come back?"

"After the rains there's gonna be a lot of rice out here. Hell," Tom admitted, "the only thing I'm sure of is that one rainy season after we're gone, the 40th is gonna be nothing but another soggy paddy field."

They didn't arrive at the first village until well after nine o'clock. Tom hadn't been pleased with the longer distances they'd been traveling lately to reach the villages in the hills north of the 40th. They had two other villages to visit that day; the furthest one would be another hour and a half away, and then three hours to get back. He wasn't happy with getting back so late, either. He didn't like being out on the flats much after five o'clock. "Hard to see things at dusk," Tom had said the first time they got back late.

At the village, Tom stayed in the jeep, using the map to figure out the quickest way to get to the other villages. David started to unload the cartons. It was hot, but he was finally getting used to it, or *acclimated,* as Cramer had said.

"How do you say *please?*"

Tom looked up. *"Please?"*

"Yeah, in Vietnamese."

Tom brushed the hair out of his eyes.

"I'm serious," David said.

"You know," Tom admitted, "I don't know. Never heard anybody use it."

"Maybe we should find out. It might make our job easier."

Tom seemed about to argue, but then changed his mind. "Okay . . ." he said.

Chapter 6

At the beginning of the fourth week, David started to take along more antibiotics. He added tetracycline, erythromycin and one of the newer synthetic penicillins that Sergeant Parker had been able to get for him from the evac hospital at the 70th. He started to hand out the medications himself. When the villagers filed past, he'd make sure those with open sores got penicillin; he gave staphcillin to the ones with abscesses. The erythromycin was used for coughs; and he gave the tetracycline to the villagers who looked chronically ill. Young and old alike received vitamin pills, and the ones who looked anemic, iron.

Tom asked an occasional question about the new antibiotics, why one was better in some cases than the other, but for the most part he ignored the additional medications, though he never challenged taking them along.

It was a very small step from trying to hand out the right pills to feeling a neck or examining a lymph node to see if it might be a tumor or abscessed. Without planning it and not quite realizing what was happen-

ing, they were turning the med caps into a mini exam
clinic.

Tom had taken his time, but he did finally find out
how to say *please* in Vietnamese. David had not pushed
the issue. The truth was he'd found out himself how to
say it the day after he had asked Tom, but decided to
wait and see if Tom would come up with it. He was
about to give in and use it when, a week later after
leaving the last village of the day, Tom had turned to
him and said, "*Lam on.* It means 'please.' "

The word had an almost magical effect. Reluctant
villagers seemed to lose their timidness, taking the pills
with something close to cheerfulness; often when he'd
say *please,* an old man or woman would lift his or her
eyes and look at him as if for the first time.

Tom was not as pleased with the clinics as the Vietnamese were. "A lot of their medicine is putting mud
and leaves on cuts. It's best," he said, "not to change
things too much."

"We aren't exactly doing heart surgery, you know,"
David answered good-naturedly.

It was their lingering at the villages that bothered
Tom most. But he said nothing about the extra time
the exams took until David started to bring along a
stethoscope. Then he couldn't control himself any
longer. "Doc, all they're used to are pills."

They were parked a few meters from the road, eating
lunch. Tom had pulled the jeep off into a small ravine
where they could be in the shade and still see the road
in both directions.

They had taken to eating their lunch on the way back
to the 40th. At times it meant holding off till late in the

afternoon, but Tom was always more relaxed heading back, and David, too, found that, as in medical school, he was more comfortable eating after all the work was done. Without any discussion, they simply continued to leave their lunches till they were on the flats again, even though with longer visits they were eating later and later.

Tom handed David a tin of chicken and opened his own.

"Pills work better," David said, "when you know what you're using them for."

Tom shook his head. "It ain't so good to stay at any one place too long."

David stretched out, resting his foot on the side of the hood. He was enjoying the silence and the sense of a day's work well done. "I don't want to get back when it's dark either."

David had mentioned Tom's concerns about the length of the trips to Cramer. "Yes," Cramer had said, "it's best to get back by evening," and then with un-characteristic candor he'd mentioned that nights in pacified areas were not as safe as they could be. But then he'd added, "Nights weren't all that safe in certain parts of the States either."

"It ain't the dark," Tom said. "Nights belong to the gooks, ain't much argument about that. It's the in-between stuff, the dawn and dusk, that's confusin', and when things over here get confusing, you can be in trouble, and real quick."

"That what Morril thought?" David asked, looking over at Tom, who was eating as mechanically as ever.

Tom shrugged. Meals for him were just something

to keep you going; another mouthful meant another quarter-mile. David had seen him in the mess hall, where the food was not so bad at times, and he ate there the same way he did out on the road. "Hard to know what the captain thought," he said.

"Sergeant Bradford told me the two of you met in the Delta."

Tom continued to eat. "Yeah," he answered, digging at the last bit of chicken.

"Bradford told me Morril wouldn't go unless Thorpe assigned you to him."

Tom took his empty tin and tossed it into the back-seat. "I'm a good shot." He wiped his hands and looked around the jeep for scraps of food or loose wrappers.

"Oh, really. A good shot, huh."

"Yeah, a real good shot."

"And Morril?"

Tom leaned back and stretched before he settled himself back into the seat. "He was special forces."

"Special forces." David was surprised.

"He liked jumpin' out of airplanes . . . he'd been a skydiver in the States and ran rapids in rubber boats, stuff like that," Tom added. "Ready?"

"You're not telling me much."

Tom turned on the engine. "Some things ain't worth spendin' much time on."

David knew the conversation was over.

Chapter 7

Every Saturday morning, Cramer went over that week's med cap missions with David. The major was not concerned with details. In fact, he didn't want to know anything about the nuts and bolts of what was going on; only the villages visited, the number of Vietnamese seen and the percentages of men, women and children.

But he appeared genuinely pleased when David mentioned that things were getting better with Tom. "If you give them half a chance, they all come around and do what they're supposed to do. The Army's okay for these kids," he said, warming to the topic. "The military teaches them a lot. I'd bet if you asked Griffen you'd find out that before the Army he'd never been more than fifty miles from his hometown. Don't kid yourself," he said. "For the poor and uneducated, the Army's a damn good deal. They see new things, go places they'd never be able to visit. I bet Griffen's been to Hong Kong and Tokyo on his R and Rs, and there's the GI Bill when they're done and the ten percent overseas savings fund. Believe me, a hell of a lot of people are going to come out of this war better off than before it, and that isn't only the ones with defense contracts. Things aren't as bad in this army as some people would like others to think."

Cramer read David's silence as agreement. They went to lunch together.

Chapter 8

The villages directly north of the 40th were the largest they'd visited. Tom looked at the ever-growing lines of Vietnamese with obvious misgivings.

"It's occurred to me," David said, responding to Tom's increasing impatience, "that you haven't been up here before."

"What do you mean?"

"When I came here, you and Morril had already been doing med caps for a couple of weeks. Then you and I began all over again, right? Redoing all the villages you'd already visited. Pretty shrewd, I mean for a country boy."

Tom actually blushed. It was the first time David had seen him looking uncomfortable.

"Don't worry," David said, clearly amused. "You're forgiven."

"These are damn long trips up here," Tom answered defensively.

"And I won't tell anyone either. Just kidding," David said, "just kidding."

David had examined a dozen villagers and was listening to an old man's chest when he called Tom over.

"Come on," David said good-naturedly. "You know we don't have all day." He motioned Tom around to the front of the jeep. "No, no, over here." He handed Tom the stethoscope. "Listen. Come on, it's just a stethoscope." Tom gave both David and the old man and then the stethoscope a wary look. "Well, go on," David coaxed. "It won't bite. Take the earpieces."

David held the bell of the stethoscope against the old man's chest while Tom slowly bent and put the earpieces in his ears. He listened for no more than a second and then, with a perfunctory nod, started to take the stethoscope out of his ears.

"Not so fast," David said. "Listen!"

Tom reluctantly bent again. He waited another moment and was about to stand when he hesitated.

"That's fluid in his lung," David said softly. He let Tom listen a little longer. "Lungs are really nothing but millions of tiny air sacs wrapped in blood vessels. When you breathe," he said, "the sacs expand and fill with air, and the oxygen in the air is picked up by the blood. If there's fluid in those sacs, when air rushes in, the fluid pops as the sacs open. That's the crackling." David moved the bell of the stethoscope to the other side of the man's chest. "See, clear. No crackles. He has a pneumonia, but it's only in the left lung."

Tom, bent over, continued to listen, his expression so intense that David found himself embarrassed. Finally he slowly straightened and started to hand back the stethoscope.

"No, no," David said. "You use it. I'll give this guy his pills. Why don't you start with that woman over there. Take my word for it, one person's lung is like any other. If there's fluid there, you'll hear it." By the time they left, Tom had examined six other villagers.

Tom didn't say a word on the way back, but it was not his usual silence. There was no distance to it. It was contemplative, more a stillness than a barrier.

"Amazing, huh," David said after a few minutes.

"Yeah," Tom admitted softly, strangely subdued. David hadn't thought about it for years, but he remembered the first time he'd used a stethoscope. It was truly like being able to see through walls. Neither spoke again until they stopped to eat.

"About that first man," Tom asked, not looking at David, pretending to be preoccupied with his tin of biscuits. "If that fluid had been on both sides, we'd have heard the same crackling all over, right?"

David was amused by the effort Tom was making to act as if nothing had happened. "Yeah," he answered as if there were nothing unusual about the question. "But most pneumonias occur only in one lung. If you'd heard fluid on both sides, you'd have to think of conditions that affect both lungs, causing the air sacs on both sides to fill. The best bets are heart failure or fluid overload." David found a small stick and drew an outline of a heart and lungs in the dirt. "When the heart fails, the blood backs up here into the lungs, into the blood vessels around the air sacs. The pressure in these vessels builds, and when the pressure gets high enough, the fluid in the vessels gets pushed out into the air sacs. You'd hear the same crackling, or rales, you heard today, only in both lungs. Kidney failure can cause a person to retain too much fluid, and eventually the same thing happens to the blood vessels and the lungs fill up, but when it's one side it's probably a pneumonia."

"Probably?" Tom glanced up at David.

"Well, there are other conditions that, like pneumonia, can affect only one lung. Cancers usually involve only one lung. They can obstruct some of the air sacs so that the airway fills with mucus and sometimes blood. You hear the rales, but those patients are usually coughing up blood by the time you hear the fluid. There are different kinds of pneumonias, too. Some are bacterial; a number are viral; a few are fungal. I assume there's a lot of TB out here. What you heard today could be tuberculosis."

"How can you tell the difference? I mean, how can you know which kind of lung infection it is?"

"Out here," David said as he rubbed out the diagram, "it's not easy. If we were in the States, we'd do chest X rays, tomograms, white counts, sputum cultures, skin tests for fungal infections, maybe even a lung biopsy. But over here," he said with a shrug, "it's penicillin or sulfa and hope that if it is an infection, the organism causing it is sensitive to penicillin."

"And if it isn't?"

"If it isn't," David said, collecting their tins and wrappers, "we might as well have plastered his chest with the mud and leaves you keep telling me about."

Tom thought for a moment. "Ain't so simple, is it?"

"It's a little harder out here. Come on," David said, pointing to the ignition. "Time to get back."

Tom started the engine but kept the clutch in. "How many years of schooling you have?"

It was the first personal question he had asked.

"Counting college?"

"The whole thing," Tom said.

"Well, four years of college, four years of medical school, a year of internship, and two years of residency —eleven years."

"Eleven years," Tom said, impressed. "Damn long time."

"That's just the beginning," David said. "When I'm done here, I'm going back to a research fellowship. That will be another three years—probably the most important three."

"But you *are* a doctor, right?"

David laughed. "Yes, I'm a doctor, all right. You're a doctor the minute you graduate from medical school. You just don't know very much yet."

Chapter 9

Within ten days, they were completely off the flats, spending all their time in the hills above the 40th. There were times when they were forced to travel below ridge lines and on occasions across a valley floor. David, despite the effort to keep his attention focused on what they were doing at the villages, couldn't ignore the difficulties they had negotiating the narrow, winding roads, some no more than ledges cut from the sides of the slopes, or their growing isolation. He hadn't realized how familiar, almost comfortable, the flats had become.

Tom had his own concerns. "With the jeep we never could hear all that much," he said as they bumped along. "Now"—he looked up at the hills around them —"we can't see all that much either."

The villages in the hills were much the same as those on the flats, only bigger; but the people were different. They were heartier than the peasants on the plateau. There was more water in the hills, the gardens weren't burned off, and there was even some rice out in the fields. The better land, though, brought with it a greater cautiousness than David had noticed among the villagers on the flats. The peasants would move up to the jeep in groups instead of lining up one by one. They took the pills, but only a few allowed themselves to be examined. There was more than enough to do, though. With the better nutrition, abscesses and pneumonias that had been so routine out on the flats were not as prevalent, but the more specific diseases began to show themselves.

David continued to teach Tom what he could. He showed him how to do a complete cardiac exam, how to palpate an abdomen for masses, and how to tell the difference between nerve and muscle damage. David only had to show Tom once and he'd have it. Soon Tom was picking out signs of disease with a skill almost equal to his own.

Their lunches became lectures. At first, David made an effort to keep his explanations simple, but as they did more exams and found more disease, the effort to restrict his discussions began to tax David's ingenuity, and out of necessity he started to go into more detail, bringing in general physiology and even pathology. Tom listened, occasionally nodding, but usually saying nothing. When he did ask a question, it was never related to what they were discussing at that moment but to something David had explained the week before. David would be talking about liver disease, and when he was done, Tom would ask a question about a point he'd made when they were discussing meningitis. The questions, though, were always to a point and so academically sound that David, who back in the States might have been irritated by such sudden changes in topic, found himself so intrigued and challenged that he didn't have time to be annoyed.

It was during those lunches that Tom would occasionally mention home, though he never really talked about himself. Tom liked his family and would speak with real affection about his parents and their farm, about hunting and fishing with his brothers and uncles.

David asked him once what he planned to do after he got back there, and Tom shrugged it off. "It ain't so good," he said, "to decide too much about things till you're there."

"You sure about that?" David asked.

"Yeah. Pretty sure anyway."

The villages became so spread out that they could only visit one a day if they wanted to get back before dark and still do the missions even halfway right. They decided to do only one village a trip, and though Tom still made it clear he was not exactly pleased with being in the hills, the decision stopped him from complaining. He did, though he refused to admit it, begin to enjoy the missions.

More than once David had to restrain himself from laughing as Tom, towering over some tiny Vietnamese, palpated for a mass or cyst with such an intense expression on his face that the villager, growing more anxious by the moment, would slowly back away and Tom, keeping pace, would continue the exam.

"It's strange, isn't it," Tom said late one afternoon while they were packing up. Earlier David had shown him how to evaluate the different muscle groups in the withered leg of a man who'd had polio. "I mean, I always thought all the cripples over here had been hit. I never figured it was something like, well, something like polio."

"There are a lot of things that can injure and hurt people besides rockets and gunships," David said, "even over here."

Chapter 10

David did see bits and pieces of the war. Twice flights of choppers moved across the horizon east of the hills, and two days in a row he and Tom watched the contrails of flights of B-52s moving in from the coast. But when David finally did find the war, it was not out on the flats or in the hills. It was at the 40th.

He and Tyler had finished morning sick call. Tyler was sitting at the microscope examining a mole he'd removed from a soldier's neck that morning. Perched on the stool, his legs drawn up, he looked like a frog with glasses.

"It's only an eighth of an inch thick," David said from across the room.

"A sixteenth," Tyler corrected without taking his eyes away from the scope. "But from the comment, I can see you do not understand the advantage of being a patient in a small socialized practice. I can say without the slightest hesitation that this mole is not malignant, because," he went on as he continued his examination, "I have personally examined every individual cell." He switched off the light and looked up, triumphant, when the screen door jerked open.

Sergeant Bradford stuck his head into the room. "Gunship with wounded, five minutes out."

Tyler didn't move, the proud look on his face fading. "Well, Doctor," he said softly, "enter the real world."

David grabbed his hat off the desk. "Plunkett's triage today, isn't he?"

"David," Tyler warned, "when they have to bring 'em down here, it's usually too late."

Plunkett was at the helipad. Brown, the air evac lieutenant, and two corpsmen were there, too. David walked over to Plunkett. "How many coming in?" The heat rose in layers off the pad.

"Don't know yet. Communications got kind of garbled."

The usual approach to the helipad was from the north, away from the buildings, then directly in over the wire.

"There it is." Plunkett pointed into the sun. David, turning, shielded his eyes and saw a small speck skimming along the ground about two miles out.

"Pretty low, isn't it?"

The chopper, its metal skin flickering in the morning sun, continued toward them. As he watched, David heard the whine of its turbines, a high-pitched whistle distorted into a kind of shriek by the thin, dry air of the flats. The chopper started to drift left. "Jesus," Plunkett mumbled. The engine sputtered and then the turbines began to whine again. The chopper gained some height but continued to veer out over the paddies, away from the base. As they watched, a tiny thread of smoke uncurled from its tail. The distance between the gunship and the 40th continued to widen.

"Why doesn't he put it down?" David asked.

"Too low and too fast," Plunkett said.

The engine noise suddenly increased in pitch. There was a frantic, metallic quality to the sound. The chopper, moving parallel to the perimeter, continued to rise. There was a moment when it seemed suspended, neither rising nor falling, simply holding its own; and then the next moment it twisted on itself and went into the ground. The main section plowed its way across the earth, while pieces of the tail and rotor flew into the air. There was a flash, transparent in the drenching sunlight, and then, as the corpsmen started to run, great curls of thick, black smoke rose up off the flats.

David started to follow, but Plunkett stopped him. "Take it easy," he said. "There's not going to be much left. Engine housings are mounted on top of choppers. When they hit the ground like that, the hot oil splashes out of the cam shaft down into the cabin. If anyone's alive before they crash, they burn to death."

Plunkett was right. It took over an hour for what was left of the main section to cool enough so they could get inside the cabin. David and the corpsmen spent that time going over the crash site, picking up the bodies that had been thrown free. Plunkett, working near the area where the chopper had first hit, called David over. He pointed to a leg lying under a section of the tail rotor. There was a tourniquet still twisted about the thigh. "Whoever they were carrying were pretty shot up. I guess the pilot figured he had to get 'em down quick."

Thorpe sent out more troopers, and by noon all the bodies, even those in what was left of the main section, had been collected. David and Plunkett walked back to the dispensary together.

"What do you think happened?" David asked.

"Hard to know," Plunkett answered. "Could have taken a round out at the landing area where they picked up the troopers, loosened or smashed something that came apart out here on the flats. It was a gunship, so either a med evac couldn't get into the landing zone or wasn't available. Gunships'll go into a hot LZ to get out the wounded if they have to and the pilots are willing to take the chance. The trouble is that choppers are complicated machines. Doesn't take much to bring one down. Hit a rotor hub, cut a hydraulic or fuel line and that's it . . . they're gone."

"Went down fast, didn't it?"

Plunkett nodded. "It always happens fast," he said. "I never told you, but I was a general medical officer with a maneuver battalion of the 25th for a couple of weeks before I got assigned here. Boy, was I glad to get out. We went out with the patrols. There were days when it was like this all the time—med evacs getting hit all over the place, gunships going down. Out of nowhere a grenade goes off, blowing away someone's leg; someone else steps off a path and a claymore levels the whole patrol. I'll tell you," Plunkett said, "this whole damn place can turn into one big surprise. I don't know. Maybe wars were always like this, but I don't think so."

David glanced back over his shoulder. The corpsmen were still picking through the wreckage.

David had taken to walking around the base after dinner, a sort of constitutional where, in the coolness of the evening, he would survey, with a proprietary air that seemed to grow daily, what had become his world. It was a time of relaxation. The day's work was done, and for the first time in years, with no articles to write or charts to review, there was nothing left to do. David usually walked first to the gate, where he'd watch the sun retreat behind the western horizon. The night of the accident, he left the mess hall and went directly to the helipad.

The sun was almost gone. The mountains, impossible to see in the bright daylight, grew close, a tiny cardboard silhouette rising off the plateau.

David sat down. The ground was like a warm blanket. He pulled his knees up and folded his arms around them. Thorpe had ordered the wreckage picked up and carried to one of the supply buildings. In the fading light, David could no longer pick out the spot where the chopper had hit the ground or where it had finally come to rest. By evening, all that remained of the crash was some scorched earth and a few furrows gouged out of the ground. Soon no one would be able to tell that anything had happened. Tom was right; one or two rainy seasons and there would be no trace of the 40th either. Yet it was not the crash that had drawn David back to the helipad, or the loss of life. He knew about death, or thought he did. He'd been dealing with it since medical school. What troubled him, what had forced him out to the pad, was not the deaths but the dying.

Another twenty seconds and they'd have made it. A quarter-mile at most; no more. It didn't seem right, to have come so close and not make it. David wondered what those on board must have thought, seeing the

40th right there in front of them, knowing they'd never get there. There had to have been a moment when at least the pilot must have known. And David had watched it all happen. He was not used to that. He had always been able to help before. Dying was something that you struggled against, that you didn't let happen. There had always been so much to do; cutdowns, blood transfusions, central venous catheters, plasma, antibiotics, respirators, cardiac massage. But there had been no way to do anything today except watch. It occurred to him that he had never seen an accident before, not one as it happened; but what astonished him even more was the realization that for all the people standing there and waiting, those men in the chopper were as alone as if they had been on the moon.

Nights in Nam come quickly. Within minutes, the sun and the mountains had all vanished, and as the sky faded to a steel gray, David found himself enveloped in the gathering darkness. He was about to get up when he heard someone coming up behind him. Whoever it was was either clumsy or was making sure he'd be heard.

"This was the last place I figured I'd find anyone." It was Tyler.

"It's cooler away from the buildings."

"It's never cool; only less hot. Sergeant Bradford says you take a walk every night. Making it a tradition?"

"For the last month anyway."

Tyler, grunting, sat down next to him. All David could see was the faint round glow of his glasses. "Anything you do over here for more than a week becomes a tradition. Does get dark out here, doesn't it?" he said dryly.

"It got dark in Saigon, too, didn't it?"

"The lights get in the way there. There's a lot of neon. Look," Tyler said softly, "I came out here to let you know that this wasn't a good day for anyone."

"I'm all right," David said.

"Yeah, but you didn't look so good this afternoon or at dinner."

"It'll pass."

"It doesn't pass," Tyler corrected. "People just get quieter. You still getting along with Griffen?"

"Huh?"

"Things still okay with him?" Tyler asked.

"Getting better."

All that separated the helipad from the rest of the plateau was the wispy luminescence of the razor wire.

"You listening to him?"

"He doesn't talk all that much."

"You should ask, then. He ever tell you why they put the 40th out here in the middle of nowhere?"

"No." David heard Tyler shift to make himself more comfortable.

"And Cramer hasn't either . . . right?"

"No, he hasn't."

"They put it here because this plateau is one of the main infiltration routes from the north into the south. We're sitting at the end of the line that runs from Hanoi to Saigon and points south and east. Last stop on the train. It's not only the main infiltration route, it's the classic one. A hundred different armies have walked across this plateau. The Mongols and Chinese used it for centuries, and everyone else since. In the fifties, when the Vietminh were fighting the French, the trail was enlarged, and the North Vietnamese have been improving it every year. It's called the Ho Chi Minh Trail after that illustrious leader of the north, but it's not a single trail; it's hundreds of miles—maybe thousands—of intertwining paths and roads and mountain passes that crisscross Laos and Cambodia."

Tyler spoke with an easy confidence that David had never noticed before. In the dark, a stranger would have thought he was a bigger man. "There are lots of exits. The one that comes out here directly ahead of us is the furthest south." Tyler hesitated. "It was the reason Morril didn't think we should be doing med caps out there. Whatever else he was," Tyler said, "our Captain Morril was no fool. He knew what he was doing out here. He was down in the Delta, out in the boonies for a while. By the time they transferred him up here he was a real savvy guy. It didn't take him two weeks to figure out the VC wouldn't let us have this plateau and the hills around it to ourselves for very long."

David didn't know what to make of Tyler's comments, particularly about the Ho Chi Minh Trail and the flats being an infiltration route. Maybe Tom and Cramer had figured he already knew, or that someone else had told him. But if Tyler was right . . . "Morril did the med caps, though, didn't he?" David asked.

"He had to; he lost the draw."

"You mean you all drew for it?" David was amazed.

"America's a democracy," Tyler said. "Besides," he went on, "Colonel Cramer knew he couldn't order anyone to do it, not after the fighting that had been going on around here before the plateau was declared a secure zone."

"Couldn't order anyone, or couldn't order Morril?"

"Well done," Tyler said. "Our colonel likes things to be orderly. A surgeon who jumps out of airplanes and can live on candy bars and chunks of hardtack wasn't exactly his cup of tea."

In the few minutes they had been talking, the moon had risen, flooding the plateau with a soft, silvered light. It was as if they were sitting at the edge of a great, motionless ocean.

"And Morril lost?"

"He lost," Tyler answered matter-of-factly.

David waited a few seconds. "Did he carry a weapon?"

Tyler laughed. "Captain Morril carry a weapon! He went out like Attila the Hun. The world's most heavily armed battalion surgeon. But to tell you the truth," Tyler added, a note of respect in his voice, "he wasn't afraid. He honestly believed in our being here. Morril might be willing to trust nature, but only because he took her on her own terms. People, though, had to be shown the foolishness of their ways, kept in place or they'd go on to ruin everything, that kind of thing."

David, lost in his own thoughts, was barely listening. "And no one cared that Morril went out armed?" he asked finally.

"David"—Tyler sounded almost apologetic—"there's no one checking on anyone out here. No one's watching. All anyone cares about is that you visit the number of villages that someone at MACV assigned to II Corps, that II Corps assigned to whoever runs this zone, who assigned it to Thorpe, who assigned it to Cramer, who assigned it to whoever is supposed to go out to the villages. Believe me, David, if this war is anything, it's a war of numbers. That's all people care about. Numbers of VC wounded, numbers of NVA killed, tons of bombs dropped, total of fighter bomber runs per day, kilos of rice captured, villages pacified, pills handed out. If you put down that you visited twelve villages instead of four, everyone would be three times as happy." Tyler hesitated. "No matter what Cramer says about Saigon, I learned a lot there. You'd be surprised," Tyler said, "what generals and colonels say when they're standing there naked bent over in front of you with a roaring case of pruritis ani, or jock itch."

Despite himself, David smiled. The thought of Tyler perched on a stool telling some naked general to bend over was something he'd like to see.

"There's no consensus on this war, David. As far as I can tell," Tyler said, "no one in the military knows what they're doing. Everyone from the top down is confused about what the objectives are; and if you don't have firm objectives, there's no way of knowing how well we're doing or even where we're going. So it's all numbers. At least you can talk about them whether you know what they mean or not. As far as I can see, the politicians are as much to blame as the generals. *Elected* officials," Tyler said, stressing the word *elected*, "don't like to decide on objectives; it's too easy to end up wrong. So they've turned the war over to their systems analysts and political scientists.

"Systems analysts?" David asked.

"Yeah, they're all over Saigon, hundreds of them. The new elite talking about cost analysis, counterinsurgency, interdiction methods, computer analysis, the light at the end of the tunnel, electronic borders. The politicians love to listen to them because no one knows what it all means; and the military has caved in to all the jargon because they don't have anything that sounds as good, or what they have is too hard-nosed to be acceptable. It's the political technicians who are running the show. A two-star told me that the head of the joint chiefs of staff doesn't even meet with the President on a regular basis. A full-bird colonel complained that in the six months he was at the Pentagon in planning and development, none of the generals in his department visited the White House or was asked to come over. All they ever got were memos from the Department of Defense that they were to increase the bombing ten percent, organize another air mobile division, or get ready to supply and equip another hundred thousand regular ground troops. It's all means and no ends. This colonel told me that all the Defense Department ever talks about is punishing the North Vietnamese. All those analyst guys think we have to do is hurt them a little and they'll cave in."

Tyler paused as if to give David a chance to absorb what he'd said. "Vietnam is nothing but a kind of actuarial game to these guys, and there's a whole group of new career officers who are learning the jargon and going along with them, telling them and the bosses— the President and Congress—what they want to hear. All an army can do—any army—is defeat an enemy army in the field, blockade a coast, and cut lines of communication and supply, and that's it. The First Air Cav can't build a country, but no one wants to hear that. Believe me. There aren't any leaders anymore," Tyler said, "only managers. Hell, the strategic headquarters for this war isn't even here in Vietnam. It's five thousand miles away in Honolulu. Take my word for it; there are still some field grade officers convinced we should be in enclaves along the coast. They want the ARVNs to do the fighting and the pacification and restrict U.S. involvement to taking on the NVA and keeping reinforcements from getting through into the south. There are a few general officers, too, who don't think that Vietnam counts or ever counted for anything. It's just something between the last great war with the Germans and the next big one with the Russians; a great chance, though," Tyler added with his old sarcasm, "to give officers combat experience for the real war that's coming. The truth, David—the Army didn't want this one. The Air Force was already saving the country with its hydrogen bombs and the Navy with its atomic subs, so when the political experts offered them this opportunity to show that wars of liberation could not succeed, they couldn't afford to say no. If they had, those bright young analysts would have chewed 'em up and spit out the pieces. The Army said yes without knowing what they were getting into. Before I left Saigon, there was information of a rather substantial increase of infiltration of North Vietnamese troops. A few of the generals in Hawaii are convinced it's only to keep units in the south up to strength, but those at MACV thought that the communists were gearing up for a large-scale conventional offensive." As Tyler continued to talk, David found himself listening. "Since we were finally going to get our chance to kill them all, they wanted the first team to be in the game. So two months ago the ARVN units were pulled out of

the front lines and sent back into secure areas, and
U.S. units were given the job of going after the communists. I don't agree," Tyler said, speaking with a
confidence David hadn't heard before. "The ARVNs
have been getting after the VC real good; so the communists, to keep things going, are sending down more
regular units, but it's only because they have to. They
don't want to take us on, or the ARVNs. I think they're
just changing strategies, that's all. All they want to do
is keep the pressure on, and the VC aren't doing it
anymore.

"The point," Tyler went on, "is that this hasn't been
a five-year war; it's been a one-year war five times." He
hesitated. "Look, it's all still just a bunch of ideas." He
sounded more cautious, as if he'd suddenly realized he
might have been talking too much, or that David didn't
or couldn't share his concerns. "I guess all I'm saying
is to take care of yourself . . . because no one else will.
Griffen knows; just listen to him. Well," Tyler said
briskly, "I've got to go."

David was about to stand also when Tyler said, "No,
stay. I do have one great physical attribute. I see excel-
lently in the dark. Don't laugh," he cautioned. "Over
here any attribute is a virtue . . . See you tomorrow."

Tyler left, the sound of his footsteps fading in the
darkness. David lay back and made himself comfortable, putting his hands behind his head. Tyler, of all
people, to turn out to be a military strategist. David had
the sense that if it had not been for the darkness, Tyler
might not have had the courage to speak. But was he
right? A few months in Saigon didn't make you an
expert in tactics, any more than a few weeks in the OR

made you a surgeon. Still, right or wrong, Tyler obviously believed what he'd said. David sighed wearily. This wasn't so easy. None of it was what he'd expected.

He stared up at the heavens. Amazing, but he could see the stars a billion miles away more clearly than he could see the edge of the helipad.

Chapter 11

"You seem preoccupied," David said.

"Preoccupied." Tom was amused by the word. "No one ever called me that before."

"Thoughtful, then."

"Yeah, maybe," Tom admitted.

As they left the base, Tom glanced over to their left, out to where the chopper had crashed.

"There's something bothering you."

Tom shrugged. He had been on patrol when the chopper had crashed and hadn't gotten back to the 40th until much later.

"It's the chopper, isn't it?"

"It's just that everyone thinks it got hit out at the LZ and went in out here."

"That's Thorpe's official report," David said. "But . . ."

"Well, there could be another explanation," Tom said.

David waited.

"It could have gotten hit out here on the plateau." David knew that he meant near the 40th. "I looked at the wreckage last night. Hard to tell a lot after they've burned up like that, but there was a groove along the outside housing of the main drive shaft and a big crack in the rotor hub. It couldn't have held together very long."

"So then it had to happen out here."

Tom sighed. "The rotor was pretty messed up; a lot of it was missing. The groove could have been from a piece of the assembly as it came loose."

"But that's unlikely since it was on the outside," David said.

"I couldn't find a hole; just the groove."

David was thinking. "But you didn't have the whole housing. The piece with the hole in it could have come off while it was still flying . . . You think it happened around here, don't you?"

"Can't be sure; besides, taking potshots at a chopper for no reason is asking for trouble."

"Thorpe told me the chopper came down from the highlands. Maybe the pilot saw something out there on the flats, troops maybe, and they shot at it."

Tom looked over at him.

"You should have told me why they put the 40th where they did. It might have explained all the road watching and smooth spots stuff. Tyler gave me a geography lesson last night, including an introduction to the Ho Chi Minh Trail."

"I would have told you if I'd seen anything."

"Tyler doesn't think we should be doing this. He thinks we should be more careful, I guess stay close to the 40th and tell everyone that we'd been to half a dozen villages that day."

"Nah," Tom said, taking David's comments seriously. "Distances don't make no difference over here. I knew a forward observer, got shot down twenty meters from the end of his own runway."

David told Tom about the rest of Tyler's comments.

"Captain Tyler say all that?" Tom said, both surprised and pleased.

"Is he right about no one knowing what we're doing?"

Tom laughed. "Pretty close, but a little too"—he looked over at David—"pessimistic."

"One for you," David said.

Tom smiled, pleased with himself. "The point is, if we catch 'em, everything works."

"What do you mean?"

"Doesn't matter what you do. Search and destroy; large sweeps; ambushes. You got to find 'em first, and then they've got to stay put. If they do, we can't lose. We almost always outmaneuver them. As far as I know, we haven't lost any major firefights recently. We did at the beginning, before we knew what to do. Now, every minute we maintain contact with the gooks, the balance swings in our favor. We can concentrate our forces quicker than they can and bring in more and more firepower."

"So we can't lose."

"Well, we can't lose, but we might not win. See, unless the gooks are surrounded, they got to decide to stay and fight. If we catch 'em, then for the most part they got to stay put, but if we don't—if we sort of stumble on 'em or it's night or close to night—they can break off the contact and fade away."

"Just a dumb Georgia redneck, huh," David said, raising an eyebrow.

"Well," Tom said, embarrassed, "it don't take no genius to figure this stuff out."

"And Tyler's worries about us?"

"Mean that we should stay around the base?"

"I don't know about Tyler's military judgments, but I think he's wrong there. We're helping, or something close to helping . . . slim stuff in the great sweep of things, but . . ." David looked ahead across the miles of desert. "Never thought I'd say something like that, but I guess when you know you can't do all that much, the little you do seems to be enough."

"Yeah, we're helpin'," Tom admitted, "but that's about it. Livin' like these people do ain't no real way to live anyway."

"Maybe," David said. "But if you have pneumonia and can't breathe, you aren't so concerned about how you live, just so you can breathe a bit better . . . basic medicine, huh," David said, feeling a little foolish about defending what they were doing. "In fact," he went on, "I doubt if you can get more basic."

"Oh, I can understand the helpin'; it's kinda nice to be able to do. I mean, it makes sense," Tom said. "It's the tryin' to help when everyone else is moving 'em out of their villages or tryin' to kill 'em that don't make sense."

"Want to stop?" David said it before he realized what he'd said.

Tom didn't answer.

"I don't either," David said. "But you're right. It doesn't make sense, but when does anything in this Army make sense?"

Tom brightened. "Now there," he said appreciatively, "you have something. I do believe you are coming around at last."

Cramer announced a week after the gunship crashed
that he'd be leaving within the month. "They'll be
sending out another surgeon," he said as if to soften
the news, "but he might not be here until after I've left.
That means that the highest officer in the grade will be
temporary hospital commander until his arrival. Of
course," Cramer added with some reluctance, "Captain
Tyler is the highest ranking officer."

"I'll consider it," Tyler said, "a stepping stone to the
head of the Department of Health, Education and Wel-
fare."

"Who we getting?" David asked, unexpectedly feeling ill at ease.

"Looks like it will be a full colonel," Cramer said with
pride.

"They upgrading the 40th?" Plunkett asked, concerned.

"No, no," Cramer answered. "No plans for that."
Tyler glanced at David and went back to his pie.

David was staring at one of Plunkett's journals when
Tyler walked into the barracks. "You're awfully quiet,"
Tyler said after a while.

"Preoccupied," David corrected. "No," he went on,
"just thinking about Cramer's leaving. I guess I've gotten used to him."

But it was a lie and David knew it. It was not that he
was used to Cramer, or even that he liked him. It was
that Cramer was leaving. He knew everyone eventually

left, but for some reason it came as a shock to see him just take off, as if nothing at the 40th mattered anymore. If you cared about something, you stayed till it was done.

"Don't despair," Tyler said. "There's a fifty-fifty chance that our next commander will be just as endearing."

"Cramer's not so bad."

"Well," Tyler said, "if it will make you feel any better, he'd be going sooner or later anyway," and then, as if reading David's mind, "No one stays to the end. Hell, no one quite knows where the end is."

The next day it was not the war that found David but David who found the war.

They had been on nothing but dirt paths carved out of the sides of the hills for most of the morning. Tom, for the tenth time in half an hour, slowed the jeep for another hairpin turn. David, engrossed in the map, was trying to figure out how long it would be before they got to the next village. They had already visited one and the other was supposed to be close to it. But, as Tom pointed out, only if you were a bird.

The jeep made still another turn. The instant they started into it, David knew something was wrong. Glancing up as they came out of the turn, he froze. He was too stunned to speak or move. The road was filled with armed troops. For a moment, it was all a terrible blur, fragments—the weapons leveled at the jeep; the armored personnel carriers off on the shoulder of the road; the tank directly in front of them—and yet he realized the jeep was still moving. Just as David saw

the small red and yellow flag of the South Vietnamese
Army, Tom pressed the gas pedal to the floor and they
were speeding down the center of the armored column,
past the groups of heavily armed troopers scattered
along the road. David, letting out a long sigh, took his
first breath in what seemed like minutes but could only
have been seconds.

"No dust to warn us," Tom said in explanation. David
tried to wet his lips, but his mouth was dry. For a few
moments, he didn't trust himself to speak. They were
soon clear of the column.

"You know," David said, "they are our allies."

"Maybe," Tom answered, "but I'd rather have the
North Vietnamese. Besides," he added moodily, "they
don't like us any more than we like them."

It was the first hint of real hostility that David had
ever seen from Tom. He looked back over his shoulder
at the quickly receding column of troops.

"Well," he said under his breath, "you may not like
them, but I'm glad they're on our side." Tom grunted
some kind of answer.

At dinner, David mentioned the South Vietnamese
unit. He didn't talk about himself, only of Tom's reac-
tion.

"They do all right when they're properly led," Thorpe
said. "The ARVNs are taking most of the casualties in
this war—three and four to every one of ours."

"Well, properly led or not," David said, "I'm glad they
were the ones on that road."

Thorpe, taking the comment as a sign of mutual
agreement, gave him an encouraging nod.

Cramer made some asinine comment about everyone being in this thing together, while Tyler and the others kept quiet.

Thorpe joined David for his after dinner walk. "In the end," Thorpe said as they reached the gate, "this is going to have to be the ARVNs' war, but right now we've got to help them out."

Chapter 12

The next morning David had the duty. There were the usual half-dozen skin rashes, so that by nine o'clock Plunkett was finishing with the forms while David cleaned up the instruments. David had kept to himself most of the morning. Nothing had happened the day before. He'd thought he'd be able to forget it, but he couldn't. Coming out of that turn had been like falling off the edge of the earth. There was no retreat; no way of changing a thing or of starting over again. He knew he'd been afraid, but it was more than that. He'd felt helpless. There had been that terrible moment when he'd known as sure as he'd ever known anything that they had already gone too far. It didn't matter that they were South Vietnamese soldiers. The point was that they could have been North Vietnamese or VC.

Something similar had occurred at the infiltration course during the last weeks of basic, but then David had dismissed his feelings as unimportant, certainly not worth pursuing at the time. Now he wasn't so sure.

It was the first time the class had worn their fatigues, and there was a certain amount of joviality as the two-

and-a-half-ton trucks pulled up to take them out to the infantry area. What little good cheer there was ended as they climbed down from the trucks. The cadre that greeted them, stone-faced and severe in their own creased fatigues and polished jump boots, were regular infantry, not the familiar, easygoing cadre of the student detachment. A number had ranger patches on their shoulders. More than one had the subdued cloth rankings on their uniforms, meaning they'd been in Nam.

A sergeant carrying a bullhorn had climbed a small ladder beside the barbed-wire entrance to the course. There was a platform on the other side of the fence with two 60-millimeter machine guns mounted on each end. David could still feel the tension.

The course was something everyone had to go through. It was routine. Yet David, like everyone else, unexpectedly found himself nervous.

The sergeant raised the microphone. "I am Master Sergeant Tate, the range master." The sergeant's voice rang out through the still air with a metallic clarity so unnatural that it riveted David to the ground where he stood. "The weapons we will be firing today are M-60 machine guns. They are fixed at a standard infiltration course height of three feet six inches. These weapons fire a nine-millimeter round that can penetrate two inches of steel and a foot and a half of concrete. This will be a live ammunition exercise. I repeat, this will be a live ammunition exercise. Out on the course, you are not to stand up. I repeat, once out on the course you are not to stand up. If at any time you find yourself in difficulty, you will remain where you are and convey that information to the soldier coming up behind you. Upon finishing the course, that soldier will report directly to me at this position. I am the only person on this range authorized to stop the firing. I and I alone am the only person authorized to clear the course." The sergeant did not ask if there were any questions.

The noise of the two machine guns was deafening. No one could hear anyone else.

David started to crawl. The machine guns were firing in short, staccato bursts. Within seconds, he was sweating. He hadn't crawled in years and it was harder than he'd thought. He'd started out too fast. The dust got into his mouth, choking him. After a minute or two, he had to stop. A charge in one of the sandbagged bunkers on the course went off. Startled, David threw himself flat. There was a moment of panic till he realized what had happened. He spit the dirt out of his mouth and, looking up, saw the bunker directly in front of him. The sharp smell of explosives filled the air. He'd been so intent on his crawling, he'd let himself come right up to the side of a bunker without knowing it. He wiped the sweat off his cheek and started to crawl again, this time more slowly, pacing himself, watching what was up ahead.

A quarter of the way down the course was the first of the barbed wire. David rolled over on his back and started to pull his way through. Halfway under, the air began to crack above him. As he cleared the last strand and turned back onto his stomach, the cracking returned. Another explosion went off, showering him with pebbles and dirt. As he started to crawl again, the snapping sound came back. This time he could feel a strange heaviness pass over him. Bullets! The thought astounded him. The machine guns fired another long burst. A split second later, the rounds passed overhead.

The sergeant's warning came back to him. If he stood up he'd be killed. The idea was outrageous. Yet the bullets had swept in again.

David reached the end of the course, exhausted, barely able to move his arms or legs. He'd leaned against the fence and looked out over the acre of barbed wire and bunkers. The machine guns continued to fire. There should have been no real danger. He'd understood that, and there was no real danger on the road— he understood that, too—but he'd been frightened both times, and, he knew, for the same reasons. Still, he hadn't shown it and he was proud of that.

Plunkett had finished with the forms and sat down at the desk to read the new issue of the *Annals of Internal Medicine* that had just come in the mail. David was thinking about asking Thorpe if the gunship might have been hit out on the flats when suddenly the metal roof of the dispensary began to vibrate.

"Choppers," Plunkett said, closing the journal, "and a lot of 'em."

They went out onto the porch together. The sky to the west was filled with helicopters.

"Big stuff," Plunkett said. "Look." He pointed to the right. A second line of choppers was coming in from the northeast. Half a dozen Cobra gunships moved beside the columns as if shepherding them along.

"I'm going down to the pad," David said.

"I'll sit this one out," Plunkett said. "Seen one chopper, you've seen 'em all."

By the time David reached the helipad, the sky was a mass of helicopters and gunships crisscrossing overhead. The noise was deafening. More choppers moved in, stacking up over the pad, hanging stationary, while those that had arrived first, engines screaming so loudly that the noise became painful, landed below them. The down drafts from the dozens of whirling rotors raised great swirls of dust that tore at the gunners and troopers braced in the open hatchways. The air grew so dense that it became difficult to breathe. A gunship suddenly materialized out of the haze, passing directly over him, the skids so close that he could see the welds on the steel tubing. More choppers arrived.

Through the haze, David could see the shadowy outlines of choppers settling onto the ground while troopers, like apparitions, jumped from the open doorways and, hunched over, scurried out from under the rotor blades. Those at the edge of the pad, emerging from the dust, began to gather in small groups. Even as other choppers moved in over them, some started assembling their gear.

Within minutes all the choppers were on the pad, and when the last engine shut down, the dust quickly settled. As the sun broke through, drenching the pad in light, David was amazed to see eight neat rows of aircraft.

The order that had materialized so suddenly out of what had seemed only moments before to be utter chaos was stunning. David looked with equal astonishment at the apron, deserted a moment before, that now held at least two hundred fully armed soldiers.

The last troopers off each chopper had carried boxes

of ammunition that they stacked alongside the landing area. A few of their comrades joined them, opening boxes and pulling out grenades and clips of ammunition that they tossed to the others.

They were all young. None of the troopers or even the chopper pilots looked older than eighteen or nineteen. Most, too, appeared gaunt. David had never seen a group of American kids who looked so lean. They had none of the robustness that you could see in the kids hanging out around any high school or drive-in movie. Many must have been twenty to thirty pounds underweight, but it didn't seem to affect them. Indeed, they reminded David more of a group of grim stevedores than adolescents, men whose lifetime of hard work had led to a kind of fitness that had nothing to do with health. Over a third of the troopers were black. The mahogany sheen to their skins reminded David of pictures he had seen of warriors on the African plains.

There was little conversation among the troops, and less joking. Some wore bracelets, but they were not very garish; only a few, unlike the pictures on television, wore beads. There were no slogans painted on flak jackets or helmets, and none wore a beard or had shaved his head. As David watched, some of the troopers moved to the shade of the nearby buildings, where they sat on the ground organizing their gear, cleaning their weapons, unconcerned about blocking paths or doorways. The majority, though, ignoring the heat, stayed out on the apron.

There was not the slightest sense of urgency to what they did, but neither was there any wasted energy. The troops stayed in small groups, as if even inside the 40th they were wary of making too tempting a target.

On the ground, a few feet from David, three troopers sitting cross-legged pumped round after round into the chambers of their sawed-off shotguns. The shotguns were wicked-looking weapons that he thought had been banned at the Geneva Convention. While he watched the troopers, the sweet smell of marijuana drifted across the helipad. Everyone had to have smelled it, but no one, neither the officers nor the NCOs who had come off the choppers nor those out at the landing area from the 40th, paid any attention.

While David watched, grenades were clipped onto web gear, ammunition was stuffed into pockets or taped to stocks of weapons, M-16s were stripped and cleaned, and all with a casualness that rendered it particularly sinister. Directly across the pad, a freckle-faced kid pulled an M-14 out of a leather case and carefully attached a telescopic sight to the rifle. A trooper next to him reached into the kid's pack and pulled out a gleaming copper-jacketed bullet. Squinting, he turned it slowly in the sun and then handed it to the redhead, who chambered the round. The trooper checked five other rounds the same way. On his face was the matter-of-fact look of the journeyman.

No one paid any attention to David; even the troopers near him acted as if he weren't there. Except for the few officers, the assault company ignored everyone from the 40th. The troopers might look up when someone from the 40th walked past, but then they would go right back to whatever they were doing.

As the troopers finished organizing their gear, they

relaxed. Some lit cigarettes or joints while others rested against their packs, helmets over their faces to shield themselves from the sun. Most sat where they were and smoked or talked among themselves.

It could have been a pastoral scene, almost summery, with heat, the soft murmur of conversation, the scattered groups of young men resting; but it wasn't. There was nothing tranquil here. It was more than the gunships and the weapons. The sun was shining and it was a languid day, but no one was at ease. It was calm, but it was a frightening calm. There was no swagger here, no arrogance, but there was a terrible tension in the air as if some kind of deadly machinery was in place there in front of him, wired and ready to go, so that all that was needed to bring it roaring to life was the turn of a key. David had never seen anything like this. He had to remind himself that these were American kids, not professional soldiers or mercenaries, but he wasn't sure he succeeded.

Turning to go back up the walk to the dispensary, he saw Tom standing at the corner of the communications building, quietly watching the troops. He didn't see David until he was walking up the path to the building. They both stood and looked at the troopers.

"Not a very talkative lot," David said.

"Well," Tom answered, "they ain't got no friends here. Besides," he added in a more sympathetic tone, "they've been out a long time. You get to look like that after a couple of weeks."

"I thought combat units go out for a few days and then get choppered back for a few days' rest."

"Nah, not these guys," Tom answered briskly. "You

know," he went on thoughtfully, "I think I recognize some of them. We had a couple of combined maneuvers with the 25th."

"Why so surprised?"

"Surprised?" Tom answered softly. "Yeah, guess I am. Those maneuvers were over five months ago." He hesitated. "I'd have thought they'd all be dead by now. Well, I got some things to do . . . See you in the morning."

David watched him walk off. As he turned for one last look, David realized that the troopers reminded him of Tom on their first day out.

The assault company left an hour later. David stepped out of the dispensary as the first choppers passed overhead. A few moments later, he heard the rattling of machine-gun fire as the door gunners, out beyond the perimeter of the base, cleared their weapons.

No one mentioned the 25th; over two hundred armed soldiers had come and gone without anyone saying a word.

After lunch, David stopped Thorpe and asked him if he knew where the troops were going.

"There's been enemy movements in the central highlands. Probably NVA; a company, maybe a regiment, no bigger. The troops here this morning were part of a combined operation to sweep the area . . . routine stuff."

David decided not to ask Thorpe about the gunship that had crashed the day before.

Chapter 13

David didn't say anything about the assault group until he and Tom were well away from the 40th. He'd expected Tom to bring it up, but Tom, like Thorpe and the others, acted as if the choppers had never been there.

"You mentioned something about those troopers having been out for weeks," David said.

"Yeah, maybe even a couple of months."

"But there are half a million soldiers over here, right?"

"Something like that," Tom answered.

"That's a lot of soldiers."

"Oh," Tom said, seeing what David was getting at. "Well, most of them half-million are in support or supply. Clerk-typists, supply sergeants, telephone operators, computer programmers. Hell, look at the 40th. A hundred and twenty guys and no one's fightin'. Then again, maybe it's best they don't."

"So what you're saying . . ."

"Only a couple divisions do any real fightin'; the 1st Air Cav, the 9th, parts of the 25th and American, the Hundred and First—that's about it, and they're all understrengthed . . . maybe forty, fifty thousand troops and that's about it. If you let those units rest, there ain't all that much left to do the fighting."

"You mean fifty thousand out of half a million do the fighting for all of Nam?"

"Yeah, ain't the half-million you thought, is it?"

"Are they enough?"

"Yeah, if all they got to do is kill gooks, but I don't think they're gonna be able to kill enough of 'em. There always seems to be more."

While they'd been talking, the road had taken them into a series of parallel valleys. They were moving up a shallow grade when Tom suddenly took his foot off the gas and let the jeep roll for a few yards until it came to a stop itself.

"Jesus," David mumbled. There was no road anymore. There was no anything. The valleys in front of them had been sheared clean of vegetation. There was not a tree or bush left standing. For as far as they could see there was nothing but craters, thousands of great, circular holes. Where one crater ended, the next began, and it went on for miles.

Tom, folding his arms across the top of the steering wheel, rested his chin on his forearms. "You can feel the ground shake ten, fifteen kilometers away when the bombs hit. MACV calls it rollin' thunder. It's scary to walk and have the ground rumblin' under your feet and not hear a thing. It ain't the detonations that do the real killin'. They make the holes. It's the concussion that flattens everything."

"Anything ever grow back?"

"Fish. In the monsoons those craters fill with water. Some of those are thirty, forty feet deep. They must have been movin' a lot of supplies down through here. Looks like the B-52s hit these valleys two, maybe three times."

David was awed by the dimension of the destruction. The very structure of the earth itself had been altered; yet for all the devastation, the craters followed the contours of the valleys, giving the destruction a kind of logic. While the valleys had been destroyed, virtually nothing outside their rims had been touched. The ridge lines and upper slopes had all been spared. The geometric precision of the devastation was as ominous as the destruction itself.

"All this was since the last rain then," David said.

"Yeah, sometime in the last four months." Tom put the jeep back into gear. "Don't worry. They don't have the B-52s we do."

They had to take the jeep back to the main road to detour around the valleys. By noon they were less than a quarter of the way to their first village, and David told Tom to stop.

"We're not going to get there much before three." He handed Tom the map. "There's another village that should be on the other side of that ridge line. We'd probably do just as well to go there. We have the kind of practice that can go virtually anywhere."

"Would seem that way," Tom said.

They turned off at the next dirt road. Neither said a word for over fifteen minutes, though David noticed Tom glancing over at him several times.

"Tell me," Tom said, "you drafted?" The question was so unexpected and so obviously genuine that David had to laugh.

"No," David answered. "I had something better—a deferment plan. A real triple treat. Keep you out of Nam, fulfill your military obligation, and practice internal medicine in one of the first-class military hospitals." Tom waited. "Then they changed the rules. It was Nam or an extra year in the Army."

"And you took Nam?" Tom, surprised, tried to make it a statement but didn't quite succeed.

"Well, an extra year was a little too much time to give up," David answered, feeling obliged to say something.

"Hell," Tom said thoughtfully, "a year over here can be a long time, too."

It took another hour to reach the village. After they'd set up and the least reluctant of the villagers had been examined and given their pills, David noticed a woman at the back of the line holding a child, four or five years old, who was too heavy for her, forcing her to shift the child from arm to arm. But she didn't move forward. She continually let others in front of her so that after half an hour she hadn't gotten one step closer to the jeep.

Finally, with the line thinning, she started to move forward, and David saw that one of the child's legs was almost twice the size of the other. At first he'd thought it was a congenital defect of some sort or a tumor, but as the woman moved closer, he saw the whole leg was swollen and covered with some kind of salve.

As the woman stepped up to the jeep, David motioned her forward. Instead of coming any closer, she held out her hand.

"No, no, please," David said in Vietnamese, motioning her on toward the hood of the jeep. The woman didn't move. David pointed to the child and motioned again.

"Doc." Tom was half a dozen feet away, examining a man's hand. "All she wants is the pills."

"The leg's infected. Look at it. It's one big abscess."

Tom motioned the man whose hand he was examining to move on. "She knows," Tom said. "All she wants is the antibiotics. There's some staphcillin up near the windshield."

"Come here," David said to the woman. The villagers walking away from the jeep stopped.

Tom straightened. "She won't show him to you," he said. "Besides, them pills'll help."

"That's an abscess. It's got to be drained. The toes are already gangrenous. There's so much pressure built up in that leg that the blood supply to the feet has been cut off. There's not enough blood flow to get any antibiotics into that leg." David started to walk toward the woman. She took a step backward.

"They got their own ways," Tom said.

"Their own ways, huh. You mean that salve. It's not doing anything for the infection or the blood supply. If the pressure isn't relieved, he's not only going to lose his toes, he's going to lose the whole leg. We've got to take him back."

The woman, not moving, continued to stare at David with unblinking hostility.

"We can't," Tom said.

"What do you mean we can't?"

"They won't treat Vietnamese nationals in Army medical facilities. Major Thorpe wouldn't let her in. It's the way it is, and besides, she won't go."

"What do you mean she won't go? She knows her child's in trouble or else she wouldn't be here."

"Believe me, all she came for was the pills."

David moved around the front of the jeep. The woman took another step backward.

"She's burned," Tom said and nodded toward the woman's legs. "Four months ago, maybe longer."

David stopped and looked at her legs for the first time.

"Luckier than most," Tom said, walking up to the jeep. "Napalm usually binds 'em up so bad they can't move." He picked up two of the bottles. The woman's eyes moved from Tom to David and then back to Tom. Suspicious, she took a half-step back toward the jeep.

"Don't give her those pills," David said. She stopped again, her eyes on David.

Tom picked up two more bottles. "She won't let us take the kid. If anyone around here don't like us, she don't," he said under his breath while he smiled at the woman. She took another step toward the jeep.

David, confused, didn't want to stay where he was, but he knew that if he moved she'd leave.

The woman stepped cautiously up to the side of the jeep. Shifting the child to her other arm, she reached across the hood.

"Those pills aren't going . . ."

But as David spoke, Tom took a short step back. It was barely noticeable, but the small movement forced the woman to reach out a little further, putting her off balance. As she hung there, Tom dropped the bottles he was holding onto the hood and grabbed her wrist. There was a flash, and the next instant a geyser of blood and pus spurted into the air. The smell of a rotten orchard engulfed them.

As quickly as Tom had plunged in the knife, he pulled it out. The child, his eyes wide, made no sound as more pus and blood ran from the wound. It had happened so quickly that neither David nor the woman had had time to move. Tom let go of her wrist, bent down, picked up the two bottles he had dropped, and handed them to her with two more. The Vietnamese who had stopped to watch continued on back to the village.

The woman, her eyes narrowed, glared for a long moment at Tom and then, pus running down her skirt, tucked the pills into her apron. Cradling the child in both arms, she followed the others. For a moment, David was too stunned to speak. Tom wiped the blood off the blade and put the knife back into his belt.

"You just might have killed him," David said once he realized what had happened.

Tom looked up and gave the retreating woman a quick, indifferent glance.

"She's got the antibiotics. Besides, she looks like she knows what she's doing."

"What are you talking about? You've turned that leg into an open wound."

"The abscess's draining."

"Draining! You don't drain abscesses by sticking them with a hunting knife."

"They ain't my rules," Tom answered. "They wouldn't have let us take her or the kid inside the 40th. They wouldn't have let you take 'em in if they were dying."

David was outraged by what Tom had done. There wasn't an intern or a medical student who'd have dared do anything close to what Griffen had done. He'd been right about him from the beginning. You can't teach a high school dropout something as intricate as medicine. David looked back at the village. The mother and child had disappeared into one of the huts. Eight or ten hours wouldn't make much difference, not unless the knife had nicked an artery or vein.

"Come on," David said angrily. "Let's clean up and get the hell out of here."

Tom seemed about to say something but, shrugging, changed his mind.

Neither spoke as they packed up. David grew angrier and more annoyed by the minute. He had let it get away from him this time, but it wouldn't happen again.

A psychiatrist during basic giving the lectures on combat exhaustion had ended the hour with one bit of advice. "No matter what else is demanded of you, remember that first and foremost you are physicians. Do what you've been trained to do, what you do best." And that, from then on, was exactly what David intended to do.

Tom tried to talk once, but David refused to answer.

Chapter 14

"What do you mean he was right?" David asked in disbelief.

"From what you told me," Cramer said, "Griffen lanced the abscess."

"If you mean he stuck a hunting knife into some four-year-old's thigh, then he lanced an abscess!"

Cramer maintained the calm, almost beatific air he reserved for discussions already settled by a directive or an Army regulation. "David," Cramer said, "look at it from the Vietnamese doctor's point of view. This is not the easiest life over here; pretty primitive, in fact. And then all of a sudden someone from another country—a richer, more technically advanced country—comes in, builds a hospital, fills in with state-of-the-art equipment, uses the newest technology and procedures and, on top of everything else, gives it away free. Now how do you think you'd feel?"

"Ted," David said, "I'm talking about a child with an abscess. What the hell are *you* talking about?"

"What I'm talking about," Cramer went on soothingly, "is policy, and policy at the highest level. We're

here in this country as guests, and we don't want to
have our hosts angry at us. They have enough to worry
about without worrying about their friends."

David was able to maintain his equilibrium only because of the blatant absurdity of what Cramer was saying. "Ted," David said, barely able to control his voice,
"in case you haven't noticed, the 40th is not exactly a state-of-the-art referral center, and in case you
haven't checked lately, there aren't any Vietnamese
hospitals out there on the plateau and there aren't any
Vietnamese doctors. There's nothing out there, fee-for-
service or free."

His comments didn't seem to affect Cramer. If anything, Cramer looked frustrated, as if David had refused to see the obvious.

"We need the Vietnamese as our friends," Cramer
said. "In a war, you can't make special rules for cities
and others for the countryside. The doctors in Saigon
and Hue, like the doctors in the States, are a power-
ful and important group of people. Now, there's a province hospital near Do Ti. They could go there."

"Do Ti! That's forty kilometers from where we were."

"David, believe me, you're doing a fine job. We all
know it and appreciate it, and that includes Med Command and MACV, but we don't want to do anything
over here to make things more difficult in the long run.
It's not going to be to the Vietnamese's advantage if we
make them too dependent on us."

"Dependent on us!" David had had enough. "In case
you haven't seen it, we're fighting for 'em."

"You haven't been listening to Tyler, have you?"

"Tyler! For Christ's sake."

"He's a troublemaker."

David was too digusted to go on.

"Where are you going?" Cramer asked.

"Don't worry, Ted. You're leaving, remember? And besides, what hospital commanders don't know can't hurt 'em."

It took David half an hour to track down the instruments and surgical packs he needed. Tyler was in the dispensary, melting wax as a base for one of his ointments, when David walked in carrying the gear. When Tyler saw the look on David's face, he put down the flask. David ignored him for a moment while he opened the packages, putting the rolls of gauze and clamps into the drawer of his desk.

"Could you do me a favor?"

"Sure."

"I'm on morning sick call tomorrow. Would you take it for me?"

"Take it for you?" Tyler said, surprised.

"I have some things to do and I don't want any shit from Cramer about not showing up. I'll be leaving early, as soon as the sun's up, but I'll be back before noon."

Tyler looked suspicious. "I know you're supposed to be winning hearts and minds," he said, "but don't you think this may be a little overambitious?"

"It's just a sick kid," David said, "nothing special, but someone's got to check on him. It won't take long."

"You sure about this?"

"As sure as I've ever been about anything." David closed the drawer and straightened up. "I'll tell you this," he said matter-of-factly. "I wasn't so confident about the specifics of what you've been saying, but you definitely got the general tone of this place right . . . real fucked up."

"I appreciate the vote of confidence," Tyler said, "even if it's somewhat provisional. What do you want me to say if anyone asks where you are?"

"Tell them I'm on a house call."

Chapter 15

David set his alarm for 5:15. He turned it off before it rang twice. He picked his flashlight off the floor and shined it around the barracks. Everyone was asleep, including Tyler. No one even turned over. He dressed and, taking two canteens, walked outside. It was just light enough to see. The mists covered the ground, drifting up around the edges of the buildings. David could hear the small sounds of the plateau carried in on the heavy morning air. It was almost cool.

David went to the dispensary, picked up the instruments and surgical packs and went back to the mess hall. The cooks did not seem surprised to see him hours before anyone else. They offered him some eggs, but he said no. Instead, he drank a cup of black coffee while the sergeant filled his canteens.

It was almost dawn when he reached the motor pool. As he walked through the gate, he stopped. Half-hidden in the shadows next to the office was the jeep. Tom was sitting behind the wheel. Damn, David thought, but he didn't fight the sense of relief that passed through him.

"Who told you?"

"Captain Tyler."

"It figures. You know, you don't have to go with me."

Tom was wearing his web gear. There were a couple of grenades hooked to the straps. "I've done crazier things," he said. "About yesterday—you get used to doing things over here quick. There ain't a lot of second chances."

David nodded and looked east at the lightening sky. "Gonna be another scorcher."

Tom started the engine. "Yeah, ain't that the truth though." They drove out into the shadows surrounding the 40th.

"Peaceful, isn't it," David said.

"It's pretty sometimes," Tom said, "but dawns can be pretty confusing. The Australians don't like 'em. We had some combined maneuvers with them in the Delta. The British taught 'em that if you're gonna be attacked, it's gonna come at dawn. Can't see all that much and the heavy air muffles noise, screws up sounds so you can't really tell where things are coming from. It's a time that gives the attackers the edge, and the gooks been around long enough to know it. If anything big's gonna happen, it's gonna come right out of this time of day and this light. All the Aussie units have what they call a 'stand to' every dawn. Everyone gets on line, even the cooks, and stays there until the sun comes up."

"And we don't."

"Every day!" Tom laughed. "Can you imagine our troops gettin' up and on line for more than a week when nothin' happens? The rangers do, but that's all. Americans got to see results."

By the time they reached the village, it was well into morning. The peasants out in the fields saw them first.

They parked the jeep in the same place they had the day before. No one came out of the huts, and the villagers in the field went back to their work as if nothing had happened.

"Don't seem too popular today," David said.

"If we ever were," Tom mumbled.

A few children came to the entrances of their huts and were quickly pulled back away from the doorways.

"What do you think?" David asked.

"They're real quiet," Tom said.

"I'll be back in a few minutes." David twisted and picked up the surgical kit. He noticed that Tom had cleaned out the back except for the tarpaulin that always covered the seat. A flak vest lay where the cartons of medicine usually sat.

"What's in there?" Tom asked.

"Lances, sutures, a syringe of penicillin. To tell you the truth, I wasn't so sure I'd be able to get her to let me take him back."

Tom, feigning indifference, waved him away.

Before David had walked ten steps, he knew something was wrong. He quickly crossed the hundred yards of open ground between the jeep and the first hut. He stopped at the doorway and, bending down, looked inside. The sunlight coming through the thatched roof sprinkled across the earthen floor. The hut was empty.

As he straightened, he saw that Tom had left the jeep and was standing on a small rise a few yards from where they'd stopped. He had put on his flak vest and was carrying his rifle.

David could see that from the position Tom had taken, he had an unobstructed view of every hut in the village as well as the fields behind it. Suddenly he understood that anyone in the village would have to have made the same observation, and that Tom must have known that, too. For a moment, David hesitated, the whole sweep of the village coming into sudden relief.

David, without quite admitting it, had stopped believing that one of anything could make much of a difference anymore. You needed teams, groups of people to get anything done. In medicine, you had to have hospitals with dozens of departments and huge laboratories. What could you do by yourself? Things were too intricate, too much had to be known and done for any one person really to accomplish anything on his own. But David understood there was more to that feeling. There was the sense of never having to decide for yourself, of knowing there was always someone there watching out for you, that somehow the process would keep you from making a serious mistake. Yet there in that blistering sunlight, complexity meant nothing anymore. It had all been a charade. No one took care of you. You took care of yourself. You did it yourself. The rest was nothing more than a kind of social faddism. There were only the two of them, and it was enough. Griffen was enough.

He watched as Tom, giving away nothing, slowly scanned the village, only his finger moving as it slowly stroked the trigger of the M-16. It was, for all its seeming casualness, not an innocent gesture. There were to be no second chances. If someone decided to start something, they would have to end it or Tom would. It was that simple and that real.

David heard a noise behind him and spun around. A

chicken scurried across the hard-baked ground. Letting out a sigh of relief, he relaxed. He was as startled by the sudden sense of responsibility as he was amazed to think that he would have come here alone.

The second hut was larger than the first and darker inside. A rug hung from the ceiling, partially concealing the back wall. David stepped inside. He waited a moment to let his eyes adjust to the dim light and then started to walk to the back. His foot sent a dish spinning across the floor. The noise startled him. He'd kicked an ashtray and bent to gather the cigarette butts. A few of the butts were still warm. Kneeling, he stopped moving and slowly looked around the hut, holding his breath. He could see a cot and a hamper behind the curtain, but otherwise the hut was empty.

He relaxed, dropped the cigarettes back into the dish and stood up. There was a small window along one side wall at the back. Whoever had been in the hut could have left through it right after they drove up. David was about to leave himself when he looked again at the hamper. Maybe there was something in it to show this was the child's hut, some of the pills or the mother's apron. He didn't want to have to go through the whole village to find out where the kid lived.

The hamper was filled with clothes. Lifting the lid, he pulled out a piece of cloth. Something metallic hit the ground. Even as he heard the sound, he knew what it was and his heart began to beat quickly. He gripped the lid and held it right where it was. In the dim light, he could see a shirt crumpled at the top of the hamper. There were epaulets on the shoulder with a single raised star.

Holding his breath, he felt along the inner edge of the hamper. He moved his finger slowly along the rough wicker surface. His finger passed over the first hinge and then touched the wire. It was hanging loose from the back of the lid. Sweating, but breathing again, David carefully lowered the lid and, bending, patted the earthen floor till he found what he was looking for. He was careful to walk backward in his own footprints as he left the hut.

Tom, who had moved closer to the first hut, remained expressionless as David opened his hand. It was a grenade pin.

"Where did you find that?" he asked.

"In a hamper in the hut. I pulled out a shirt and it fell out. The shirt had a star on the shoulders and there were cigarette butts in a dish. Some were still warm."

"Do what I say," Tom said. He took the pin and with an exaggerated gesture threw it into the dirt behind him. "Point to the first hut," he whispered.

David pointed. Tom shook his head and pointed to a hut at the opposite end of the village, but as he pointed David saw that he flipped the M-16 to automatic.

"Stamp your foot like you're angry. Now, when I push you, start walking back toward the first hut, take half a dozen steps, then stop like you've changed your mind, and then head back to the jeep. Don't pay any attention to what I do. Just get back to the jeep."

Tom suddenly shoved David, pushing him backward. Before he could recover, Tom had turned and walked over to where he'd thrown the grenade pin. He bent as if he were looking for it. David had only taken three steps when Tom yelled, "Over there." The shout startled him, but he kept moving. He stopped, and as he turned he saw Tom out of the corner of his eye, his rifle in firing position, running off in the opposite direction. Within seconds, they were a dozen yards apart.

"Captain!" David turned around. Tom, near the last hut, pointed toward the vegetable garden behind the village. "Up there," he yelled. "I think I see 'em," and he started to run past the huts toward the garden.

David couldn't see anyone as he kept on toward the jeep. He climbed behind the wheel and, his hand trembling, switched on the engine. A few minutes later Tom reappeared, coming up from behind the jeep. He had circled the village. As Tom got in, David put the jeep into gear and, even before he settled into his seat, started to drive away. They drove for a few minutes. David tried to collect himself.

"You thought they were still in the village, didn't you," David said, trying to sound calm.

"Yeah"—Tom had taken off his web gear and sweat-soaked flak vest—"or not very far away." He threw them both into the back. "They might even have still been in the hut. There's probably a hundred miles of tunnels around here; could have been a trap door in the floor. Cigarettes don't stay warm all that long. Sorry I pushed you, but if they was watching I wanted 'em to think we were arguing. Most people wait until an argument's over before they decide anything themselves. You okay?" he asked.

"Yeah, I'm fine."

"You don't look it."

"No, I'm okay."

"Look," Tom said, "nothin' happened. It ain't the first

grenade that goes off that should worry you," he said good-naturedly, "it's the last."

"It wasn't a dud," David said. "They didn't have the time to set it up right. When they saw you get out of the jeep, they must have decided they'd better leave. There was a piece of tape holding the wire down to the back of the hamper. It came loose. If it had stayed in place, there wouldn't have been any slack; the wire'd have pulled out the lever when I lifted the lid and the grenade would have gone off. You scared 'em. I mean it. No," he said, stopping Tom from interrupting, "it's the truth and you know it."

"Hard to know that," Tom said, "but there is one thing that bothers me. They might not have expected us to come back today, but there sure as hell wasn't no reason to rig a booby trap. These villagers know the war; they know the real thing when they see it, and we ain't close to the real thing."

"Meaning?" David asked.

"Maybe whoever they were that set it up ain't from around here. It could have been a kind of reflex thing. See some U.S. troopers and get rid of—"

David reached over and put his hand on Tom's shoulder, stopping him from talking. "Thanks," he said. "No, I mean it," he said softly. Tom seemed to blush. "To tell you the truth," David went on, "whatever the reason, I'm glad it didn't go off."

Tom laughed. "Yeah," he said, "me, too. Believe me, if the damn thing'd gone off, they wouldn't have let me get away either. Nothing starts until the trap is sprung. It's one of the rules."

For the rest of the trip back to the 40th, they were both silent. Neither mentioned the woman or the child.

Chapter 16

"Going out again?" Tyler asked as David put away the last of the gear from the trip. Tyler noticed that it hadn't been used. "Only asking," he added quickly, "in the event that I have to explain things to our leader a second time. He's rigid, but not dumb."

"No," David answered. "But if I do, I'll let you know in plenty of time."

"Good. Cramer made it perfectly clear that schedules are schedules and if they are not adhered to they are no longer schedules. There are times when he can be remarkably insightful." But he stopped talking when he realized David wasn't listening.

David kept busy the rest of the afternoon, but toward the end of the day, the events of the morning caught up with him. He could shake everything; the foolishness of going back to the village, not understanding what the warm cigarette butts meant, even opening the hamper. What he couldn't put out of his mind was the fact that except for Tom, some incompetence on the part of whoever had set the grenade, and a few extra seconds, he'd still be in that village, probably buried by now with no one ever knowing what had happened to him. It was so bizarre as to seem almost funny; and, indeed, he might have laughed if he hadn't remembered the sudden dryness in his mouth as he waited for the grenade to go off. Whatever had saved him, there hadn't been much of a margin.

Instead of going to dinner, he walked out to the helipad. Nothing had changed from the night he'd talked to Tyler, and yet everything was different. The sky, the razor wire, the distant mountains no longer seemed to be part of the same landscape. They were isolated, separate one from the other. The order was gone. What had then been a magical landscape was now harsh and unbalanced. Nothing fit together. He saw only edges and boundaries. Even the moon, hanging there on the horizon, looked flat and out of place, as if it were no more than an intruder. It was as if he were looking at one of those puzzles in which when you see the vase you cannot see the faces. He was too weary to fight the new perception, though he had the sense that had it been lighter, he could have picked out a bird a mile away.

It seemed as if years had passed since his talk with Tyler. How long had it been since the chopper crashed? Christ, he thought. Their deaths had made no more sense than his or Tom's would have. There was no reason for them, unless, David thought for a moment, it was simply because they were there. Maybe that was the answer, just being there. It had all been so innocent. He had chosen Vietnam because the extra year would have held back his career. Not an unreasonable decision. The problem was he hadn't known what he was deciding. Suddenly he realized he'd been a fool about more than just going back to the village.

At breakfast, Cramer said that he would be leaving in nine days. "Since there is no replacement as yet, Captain Tyler will be acting hospital commander until my replacement arrives. The colonel," he added pointedly, "should be here within the next three weeks. I'll be meeting with Captain Tyler to prepare for the transition. If any of you have items you'd like brought up, put them in writing and give them to me before tomorrow morning."

Breakfast ended without Cramer saying a word about David's absence from the 40th. On the way out of the mess hall, David pulled Tyler aside.

"I was a little tired when I got back yesterday," he said. "I just want you to know I appreciate what you did."

"There's no need . . ."

"There is," David said seriously. Tyler nodded; a small, appreciative smile flickered across his face. They walked together to the dispensary.

"Tell me," David said, "about Morril. He and Tom did more than just meet in the Delta."

"There were rumors . . ."

"Rumors?"

"A few days after Morril got here, he was in the dispensary cleaning out his duff kit and spilled some pills. They weren't exactly government issue."

"What were they?"

"Cytoxan."

"Cytoxan!" David repeated. "That's pretty deadly stuff. I mean for out here."

"They were whoppers, too. Five-hundred-milligram capsules."

"They're used for killing cancer, or for patients whose immune system you want to poison."

"And some severe skin problems; that's how I learned about it."

"But why?"

"There was some talk in Saigon about physicians working with military intelligence."

"And you think Morril worked for them. But why the Cytoxan?"

"Well, it's tasteless. You can dump fifty or sixty into a bucket of water and no one would know they were there."

"And it's excreted by the kidney and concentrates in the urine."

"Yeah."

"And one of its complications is that in high concentrations it causes the bladder to hemorrhage with no way to stop the bleeding except to surgically remove the bladder."

"Pretty dramatic," Tyler said, "to bleed to death pissing blood. Everyone knows."

"But Morril wouldn't have needed Tom for that."

"Dangerous place, the Delta, especially at night. It would be better to go out with someone like Tom. Don't get me wrong, Morril was a nice guy, but as far as he was concerned, it was them or us. And I mean," Tyler said without any hint of sarcasm, "just that . . . them or us."

"You think Tom knew?"

Tyler didn't have to answer.

"Well," David said, "it must have given him a unique perspective on American medicine."

Chapter 17

The next day Tom sought David out and found him in the dispensary. David was alone.

"Well," he said when Tom walked in, "don't tell me you have a rash."

"No," Tom said. "I'm okay. I was just wondering how you were doing."

"Me?" David answered, surprised.

"You were real quiet comin' in yesterday."

"I'm okay."

"You got to put things like that behind you."

"A little like getting back on a horse after you've fallen off."

"Nothin' happened," Tom said seriously. "We'll just be more careful."

"I'm all for that."

"I got to go," Tom said. "See you tomorrow mornin'."

"How about lunch."

"Lunch?"

"Any difference here or out on the flats?"

"No," Tom said. "Guess there isn't. Sure, why not. See you at the mess hall."

Chapter 18

As usual, the jeep was ready when David arrived at the motor pool.

"I figured we'd stay on the flats for a while," Tom said, "till things get sorted out. We can see more out here than in the hills. And hear more, too . . ."

But even though they could see for miles, David watched everything a bit more closely than usual, and when he dozed off it wasn't so completely that he ever stopped listening. It wasn't quite like getting back on a horse. David wasn't exactly afraid, but he wasn't as relaxed as he'd been before, either.

At lunch, Tom mentioned Cramer. "I hear they're replacing him with a full colonel."

"Maybe only a lieutenant colonel; Cramer was a little vague. Not impressed either way, huh?"

"Nah. All that rotation stuff does is screw up morale, doesn't matter whether it's a full bird or a major. Everyone coming and going. Officers, NCOs, enlisted men. You can't keep anything straight. One CO wants this and the next one wants that. It's a mess. Hell, for all we know, this new colonel won't like gooks or will think med caps aren't worth a pile of shit and work on some way to cancel 'em or, like Captain Tyler said, just have us pretend we're goin' out, dump the pills and have us do somethin' else. But," he added, "you got to look at the bright side—the bad ones leave, too. So I guess it all evens out in the end."

"And if everyone stayed?"

"Stayed?" Tom shrugged. "I heard some officers at the 9th talk like that once, about what would happen if everyone had to stay till the end." Tom raised an eyebrow. "They were sure we'd win in a year or see a mutiny."

"And Captain Morril?"

Tom didn't hesitate. "The captain believed that the one-year tour was nothin' but a way to keep the enlisted troops in line. He figured the politicians and the generals were afraid to keep everyone here till it was over, so they decided that no one would scream too much about one year." He gave David a knowing glance. "Besides, it gives the Army a chance to have all its field grade officers get some combat experience."

"That your idea or Morril's?"

"Mine."

"For the next war?"

"It ain't for this one," Tom answered flatly. "As soon as they figure out how to get it done right, they're gone."

"Get it right?"

"Have us get them without them gettin' us."

"And the rest, the enlisted men—would they stay?"

"A lot of guys would, and stay till the end, if there was an end. We can beat the north, but I guess there

ain't no way to make 'em surrender, not with the
Chinese and the Russians helpin' 'em. We probably
can't even make 'em back down, but like the captain
said"—David knew he meant Morril—"all we're supposed to do is save the south; we ain't supposed to beat
the north. The captain didn't think winnin' meant the
other side had to surrender; all they had to do was give
up."

"And you agree?"

"Well, we could seal off the infiltration routes from
the north, close off the Delta, take the casualties that
all that would mean and let the south deal with the
nation building, stuff like these med caps, on their
own. Hell, we're down here gettin' killed anyway.
Might as well die for somethin' that makes sense."

Chapter 19

For the next few days, they ignored the schedule and stayed out on the plateau. Tyler had been right. No one cared.

David had had trouble sleeping. He thought it would pass, but it didn't. He'd lie there at night thinking, though his thoughts had little to do anymore with what had happened at the village or with the helicopter. He had put those two events behind him, but he did wonder where else he'd been foolish and either not known enough or missed the obvious. He thought of what Tom had said the day after they'd stood at the helipad watching the assault troops of the 25th, not about the small number of troops actually fighting but about the casualties. He'd stayed awake wondering about that for two nights until finally he asked Tyler about the numbers wounded. Tyler said he'd heard it was up to a hundred thousand, at least since the buildup two years before. If Tyler was right about the numbers of casualties and Tom was right about the small percentage of troops actually doing the fighting, then the risk of being killed or wounded in Nam had to be astronomical. Sixty thousand troops fighting, fifty thousand or so casualties in a year. In one year just about everyone in a combat unit had a good chance of being hit.

At the end of the week, he was lying in bed, as usual half in, half out of sleep, when he heard the sounds of an approaching chopper. He lifted his arm and looked at his watch. The dial glowed feebly in the dark. Three-thirty. The roof started to vibrate.

He sat up, quickly pulled on his pants and shoes and went outside. As he passed Cramer's cot, he noticed that it was empty.

By the time he reached the helipad, his eyes had become accustomed to the darkness. He could see the outline of a chopper sitting near the edge of the pad. No one was there. He was about to go back up the path to the dispensary when he saw the shadowy shape of a second chopper further out on the pad. Two, he thought. He must have been asleep when the first one came in. He hurried up the path.

He saw the red glow of the cigarettes as soon as he passed the communications building. They flickered in the air like two tiny beacons. It was only when he was a few feet from the dispensary that he saw the troopers who held them. Bandoliers of ammunition crisscrossed their chests, the bullets glistening in the darkness. They were wearing helmets. David couldn't make out their features, but there was a heavy, musty smell about them, as if they had been wet for a long time.

The taller one took a long drag. His unblinking eyes reflected the tiny flare of light as if they were glass.

"What's going on?" David asked.

The cigarette tips dimmed and they were back in darkness again.

"You work here?" The voice, like the eyes, had a metallic quality.

"I'm one of the doctors."

"Our buddy's been breathing fast for three days. Couple hours ago he had a fit. The lieutenant called in a med evac."

"Us four been together from the beginning." The shorter one was talking. From the tone of his voice, he might well have been speaking of the beginning of the world. "We come along to be sure everything's okay."

"He's inside?" David asked.

"Yeah."

"I'll see what's happening."

Neither the tall one nor the short one moved. David had to walk around them.

Sergeant Parker was at the desk. He glanced up as the door swung open, looking relieved when he saw who it was.

"Sorry, sir, I thought it might be one of those two geniuses outside."

"I told 'em I'd check on what's going on."

"You talked to 'em?" he said, surprised.

"A little. What's wrong?"

"They tell you they requisitioned a supply chopper? Told the pilot they'd kill him if he didn't bring 'em here to see what was happening to their buddy."

"That's the second chopper out on the pad?"

"Stole it right out of the landing zone."

"Does Thorpe know?"

"No, sir." The sergeant looked pained. "Maybe it was too dark for you to see, sir, but those guys are armed to the teeth, and believe me, they aren't the kind that listen. Besides, there's another genius or two down at the helipad right now making sure the choppers stay requisitioned."

"Where's the trooper?"

"In the treatment room with Colonel Cramer, and he ain't exactly a Mr. IQ either."

"What was wrong?"

"Something about a friend he sees all the time, talks to him, things like that."

"And the friend?"

"If you can believe the two crazies outside, at this moment he's in a bag in the mortuary at the 70th."

"Dead?"

"Yeah, and for the last week, maybe longer. They've been in a kind of running firefight, so they ain't so good on dates and times."

"What about the trooper?"

"Well, I ain't heard no shots yet."

"What?"

The sergeant lifted his arms in a hopeless gesture. "What could I do, sir? He wasn't about to be disarmed."

"And Cramer?" David asked, looking down the hallway.

"There wasn't much he could do, either. Oh, sir," the sergeant warned, "I don't think I'd go down there just yet." He pointed to the tray on the side of his desk. It contained a vial of medicine and a half-filled syringe. "He ain't got his Thorazine yet."

"How long have they been in there?"

The sergeant looked at the clock over the door. "Going on fifteen minutes."

"Don't let anyone else down the hallway."

David hurried down the corridor before the sergeant

could stop him, slowing as he neared the treatment area. He could hear voices coming from the first examining room. He slowed the last ten feet and then edged forward to the half-open door.

"I'm telling you, I want to call my parents."

Cramer was sitting on a stool. He was wearing slippers, and his hair wasn't combed.

"You're tired." Cramer was trying to be casual, but he looked anxious.

"I said I—want—to—call—my parents."

The trooper's boots were visible through the doorway. They were muddy, and the tops were torn. David could just see the barrel of the M-16. It was pointed toward the floor but in Cramer's direction.

"And the dizziness?"

"Dizziness . . . shit," the trooper said angrily. "That all anyone fuckin' cares about? I get dizzy, that's all!"

"Do you breathe fast before you get dizzy?"

"Breathe fast? How the fuck do I know?"

"It's important," Cramer persisted.

"Yeah." The trooper's voice sagged so that David could hardly hear it. "I breathe fast."

He could see Cramer relax. "That's called *hyperventilation*." David moved closer to the doorway. "When people get nervous, they breathe fast. That decreases the carbon dioxide in the body, changes the acid concentration in their blood, and they get dizzy."

David couldn't believe that Cramer was discussing the physiology of acid-base balance.

"When the acid changes, the composition of chemicals in the brain changes and —"

"So what!"

Cramer was suddenly more cautious. "If that kind of breathing goes on long enough," he said, "people get faint. They might see things, and if it goes on too long, they lose consciousness and can even have a seizure."

"What the fuck does that matter?"

"Well," Cramer went on quickly, "if you're the one breathing rapidly, you can begin to see things that aren't there, and a lot of people don't know they're breathing fast until someone points it out to them."

"What are you talkin' about?"

Cramer sat up straighter.

"The gooks are out there trying to waste us and you talk about carbon something."

The chair squeaked as it moved. Cramer stiffened.

"You're a fuckin' lifer, aren't you? You ain't no real doctor!"

"No, no," Cramer said, trying to sound cheerful. "I'm a draftee just like you, but I'm still a real doctor." He shifted his feet off the stool. There was a sharp click as the rifle barrel disappeared from David's view.

Cramer, his eyes wide behind his horn-rimmed glasses, inched his way back onto the stool. David knew Cramer was a little dense, but he hadn't realized he was so stupid. Still, he might not have known about the two riflemen outside or the stolen chopper. He must have already been in the dispensary when the second chopper came in and figured it was just another evac. David moved a half-step closer to the door.

"Tell you what," Cramer said, his nerve returning. "You can call home. But first I think you should get some sleep. You don't want to call home and talk to your parents when you're all tired and exhausted now, do you?"

"And Frank. What about Frank?"

"Frank?"

Christ, David thought, Cramer must have walked into the room without finding out why the kid had been evaced in. But from the look on his face, he'd finally figured out that both he and the kid were in more trouble than he'd realized. Standing there, David went through the options. There weren't many.

"Frank!" the trooper mimicked angrily. "What's he gonna do when I'm asleep, huh? Did you ever think of that? What kind of doctor are you anyway?" The trooper was working himself up. "Who's gonna take care of him, huh? Think I'm gonna let some candy-assed lifer do that? No, not after all we've been through . . . not a chance." David could hear the trooper shift his position. "Now get the fuckin' phone." The voice was sinister.

It wasn't a request but a command. Cramer, to his credit, tried to maintain his composure. But David could see that Cramer didn't know what to do and that it was taking too long. He had the same feeling he'd had standing at the jeep the day Tom had used his knife on the child; the sense that it was slipping away.

The trooper's chair moved. David saw Cramer freeze. He moved forward, slamming open the door. There was a sharp crack and the rifle spun past Cramer.

"New evac coming in, Colonel," David said, quickly stepping into the room. Cramer, startled, looked at him, his eyes so wide they seemed to fill his glasses. "They need you in the OR right away. Med evac chopper'll be here in a few minutes." David turned. The rifle was lying on the floor. "You're Frank's friend, aren't you?" he said in the same breath. The soldier, a short, swarthy kid with pinched cheeks, stared up at him.

"He sent word with your two buddies—a tall guy with a beard and a short, stockier fellow. They're outside. Wanted to make sure you're okay. Said you've been together a long time. You won't need that," David said, walking across the room and picking up the rifle. "Anyway, they told me to tell you they've got to go back and that everything's okay. They'll come to get you in a couple of days. Sergeant Parker, the sergeant you saw at the desk, will be here in a couple of minutes. It's okay; your buddies checked him out. He's going to give you something that'll help you relax. The one with the beard, what's his name?"

"Pete," the trooper mumbled.

"Well, Pete says they need you rested when you go back. Says you've been pushing real hard and could use some rest." David turned back to Cramer. "Come on, Colonel. Sergeant Parker will be right in; you've got to get back to the OR."

Cramer slowly got off his stool. "Hurry, Colonel," David said sharply. Cramer, coming out of his daze, quickly followed David into the corridor. He was about to speak when David angrily motioned him to be quiet and to follow him. Back at the desk, he handed the M-16 to Parker. "You can give him his Thorazine now."

"You scared the hell out of me back there," Cramer said when the sergeant left, "rushing in like that . . . damn, but . . ."

"You had everything under control, right? Is that it?" David asked coldly.

"Well, he was a little shakier than most, but a few more minutes and he'd have been okay."

"Tell me," David said, "only out of curiosity, what were you going to do? Sit there? Fake a telephone call to the States? Or wait the half-day till maybe a call could get through? Those two guys I mentioned in the treatment room—I didn't make them up. They're right outside and they can barely tell the difference between me and you and the VC. They stole a chopper, Ted, right out of their LZ, and some more of them are out on the pad right now holding the crews at gunpoint. In the States stealing helicopters is a felony. I assume over here it's a court-martial offense. You were running out of time. Frank's been dead a week. This kid was hallucinating, Ted, and he had a loaded gun pointed at you. He didn't want to hear about blood gases or hypocalcemic seizures."

"And he could have pulled the trigger when you barged in like that!"

"But he didn't, did he? And you're safe and he's got his Thorazine. You want to talk to his friends?" David asked. Cramer shook his head. "I didn't think so."

David walked back outside. The two troopers had moved away from the front of the dispensary into the heavier darkness away from the building, but David could still make them out by the light coming past him through the open doorway. The night closed in again as he shut the door and walked over to them.

"Your friend's going to be all right," he said. "But he'll be sleeping for a while."

"We should all be sleeping," the shorter one answered, "but he's the one seeing dead people."

"That may be because he's exhausted. We're giving him something to help him rest."

"What?" the tall one asked.

"Thorazine; it's a tranquillizer."

"A tranquillizer." For the first time, the trooper sounded interested. "You send them back with the shit?" he asked. "The dope, man. Does he go back with the dope?"

"It's not dope, it's a—" David caught himself. He was beginning to sound like Cramer. "No," he said. "It's just used here, but it'll keep him sleeping for a couple of days."

"And when he wakes up, what happens if he freaks again? It was a shitload of trouble getting him here. We might not be able to do it again."

David wished he could see the two of them better. It was like talking to ghosts.

"The drug's only to help him sleep. After he wakes up, we'll be able to tell whether he's been seeing his friend because he's been pushing too hard and is just exhausted or because he really has cracked up."

"How you gonna tell that?"

Surrounded by darkness, barely able to see, it made no sense to pretend.

"Look," David said, "I'm not a psychiatrist; none of us at the base is. All we know about what's going on with your friend is what we've picked up over here, with some help from what we learned in the States. If he's still seeing things after he's rested, then it's something more than exhaustion. We'll do the best we can."

"How long?"

"How long what?"

"Between the time he wakes up and you knowing if he's okay."

"Depends on how much of the shit they give him, right?" the shorter one asked with a kind of malevolent humor, as if he and David shared a secret. But the raw hostility was gone. "You know," he added, "we could have doped him up ourselves."

"A day or two," David said.

"You be taking care of him?"

"I'll be one of the doctors."

"And if he's still seeing things?"

"We'll evac him to the 70th. There's a chance then that he's real sick, maybe even psychotic."

"Psychotic!"

There was a moment of silence. "Did you hear that?" the shorter one said, amused. "Psychotic . . . shit. Doc," he said, "if you think just seeing dead people is psychotic, then what's the real stuff?" They both laughed.

The dispensary door opened and the tension returned with the light as Cramer stepped into the doorway.

"Come on," the short one said to his friend. "Let's get out of here. Todd'll be okay. Ain't no one here going to hurt him . . . Psychotic." Still laughing, they both walked away.

Cramer stepped up beside David. "They going?" he asked nervously.

"Yeah, they're going."

"Sergeant Parker told me what happened."

"How much Thorazine did you use?" David asked, continuing to look in the direction the two troopers had taken.

"Three grams, why?"

"That's a lot, isn't it? Normal dosages are somewhere around five hundred milligrams."

"Normal levels don't work. Look," Cramer said, changing the subject, "I don't want you to get me wrong about what went on in there; I appreciate what you did. It just kind of caught me by surprise, that's all."

Through the darkness David could still hear their laughter, thin and distorted by the misty night air. "Ted," he said wearily, "where you think you've been all these months? Maybe it *is* time for you to go home."

A few minutes later when David reached the barracks, the choppers had already started their engines.

Chapter 20

"Yeah, I heard the two of 'em come in. Damn, stealin' a chopper! Now that," Tom said, "takes real balls."

"I checked on the kid before breakfast," David said, putting the canteens into the jeep. "He's still asleep. Tyler's on sick call today, so he'll be watching him. The kid will probably be out for at least another forty-eight hours, maybe longer. Three grams of Thorazine can act like four or five when you're dehydrated, and that kid was real dried out."

"Just took the chopper, huh, and right out of a hot LZ? Not bad, not bad at all," Tom said appreciatively.

David walked around the back of the jeep and got in. "You don't see anything wrong with it, huh?" Tom looked at him. "All right," David admitted, "I guess I don't see much wrong with it either."

Tom started to laugh. David began to laugh himself.

"You know," he said, still laughing, "you should have seen the look on Cramer's face when I barged into the room. Damn . . . I'll tell you, it was something. Can you imagine," David said, trying to be serious, "explaining the pathophysiology of hyperventilation to a kid holding a loaded gun on you, and doing it with a straight face?"

But being serious didn't work. It only made it more ridiculous, and they both started to laugh again and kept laughing until all the heat and worry were forgotten, and they drove out of the 40th as relaxed and comfortable as they'd ever been with each other.

"There's no doubt you can get really dingy out here," Tom said a few minutes later.

"Talking about Cramer, the kid or his friends?" David asked.

"All of us," Tom said without the slightest hesitation.

"Yeah," David admitted, "that's true. What happens when they get back?"

"Back?"

"Like this kid, say he's okay. What happens when he gets back to his unit? During basic we only had an hour lecture on military psychiatry—not a hell of a lot—and they made it sound pretty simple. No one calls it *shell shock* anymore like they did in the first world war or *battle neurosis* like in the second or Korea. Now it's *combat fatigue*. They think it's all exhaustion, so you let them sleep or put them to sleep, and when they wake up they're fine, and if they're not the idea is they were in trouble before the Army and the stress of combat or whatever pushed them over the edge. Since the majority of those who freak out aren't supposed to be crazy, just tired, all you have to do is let them rest. I know," David said, seeing the look on Tom's face. "But it seemed to make sense in Texas. You don't evac them out of the combat area so that when they wake up the guilt they're feeling because they left their units doesn't become fixed and end up a bigger problem than what caused them to be evaced out in the first place;

that's supposedly the reason you send them back to their units so quick. Simple, huh? What does happen when they get back?"

"Never gave it much thought," Tom said. "Doesn't bother anyone. Besides, it's hard to keep track of who's freaked out and who hasn't. When there's a firefight or you're just taking incoming, everyone that's hit or sometimes just bleeding gets evaced out together. There ain't no time to figure out who's really bad off and who isn't. Sometimes a lot of blood ain't nothin' and a little wound that you figure was no more than a scratch ends up killin' someone. Things get even worse when contacts come one after the other. Hard to tell how bad someone's wounded, so when they come back you never know exactly what's happened to 'em. There's no way to tell who's freaked out and come back and whose wound didn't amount to much."

"And it doesn't worry anyone?"

"Having guys freak out and then come right back? Nah," Tom said, unconcerned. "It don't take all that much to pull a trigger."

"That's the point," David said. Tom looked over at him. "There's no medical follow-up. Once the trooper steps off the chopper, that's it; no one watches him. Maybe his commander doesn't even know why he got evaced out. No one ever checks to see if he's the one who steps left when everyone else steps right or walks into a booby trap that everyone else missed."

Tom thought for a moment. "You mean the docs don't know if they're doing it right?"

"Hard as hell to figure out who's mentally ill and who isn't in a couple of days, much less an hour or two after they wake up from being zonked with a tranquillizer. The Army does get what it wants, though. The troopers get sent back to their units, and like you said, it doesn't take all that much to pull a trigger. You need a follow-up in medicine to know if what you're doing is right."

"Damn," Tom said, "you do take things down to their parts."

"I'm a little behind," David said dryly. "Someone in the Army's already done it."

David was shielding his eyes. While they'd been talking, he'd been looking at a rock formation out on the flats. "Hold it," he said.

Tom, putting on the brakes, stopped the jeep.

"See that formation over there, the one that looks like a boat?"

Tom leaned past him. "There's something different about it from two days ago. I think something moved." Tom put the jeep into neutral, leaving the motor running. "Let's go see." He grabbed the M-16 from under the dash. They walked together across the rocky ground.

There was a six-inch piece of cloth snagged on one of the rocks. Tom pulled it off. It was faded by the sun, but they could still see its basic khaki color.

"I might have missed it last time," David said. "It could have been here for weeks."

"Yeah, maybe." Tom, walking around, looked at the ground.

"What are you looking for?"

"Hard to tell. The ground's pretty messed up around here. Could mean a lot of people moving through." He looked up at the sun. "Nice place to keep out of sight in during daylight. Well, come on," he said. "There ain't nothin' else here." Tom put the cloth back where he'd found it. "You know," he said, "it was really something to spot this. I mean it."

David was pleased. "Thanks," he said softly. "I appreciate the vote of confidence."

Chapter 21

David hurried to the dispensary as soon as they got back from the villages and unloaded the jeep. Tyler was there. The patient was still asleep, but he had an IV running.

"Figured I'd improve his hydration while he slept," Tyler said. "I heard about what happened last night. You might have saved our soon-to-be-departed commander from significant bodily injury."

"Hard to know," David said.

"Oh, really," Tyler commented dryly, "you may not have found out yet, but our patient and his friends aren't your average run-of-the-mill combat riflemen. They're rangers, and what you saw last night was all that was left of their unit. They'd been scaring a lot of people, ours and theirs. As for saving our commander, we'll never know, will we. Part of the problem of dealing with negatives, things that never happen. You can't be sure. But then again," he said with a slight shrug, "if you'd decided not to bust in . . ."

"I guess I was worried about the kid, too," David said.

"A reasonable concern. Ted is not at his best when

dealing with the unusual or the bizarre. I infer from all the dust on you that you came to see your patient before you cleaned up."

"Right."

"See, you do get an instinct for these things after a while."

The trooper was asleep. The IV solution hanging above the bed was running slowly through the tubing into his arm. David checked the composition of the bottle. It contained exactly the right concentration of electrolytes for a dehydrated patient.

"Not bad for a dermatologist."

"Well," Tyler answered, trying to act indifferent, "sooner or later everything connects to the skin."

David didn't have to ask who'd washed the trooper and shaved him.

Chapter 22

"Teeth!" Tom exclaimed.

"Sure, why not? If there's one thing we can do that's worthwhile and that might last for more than a couple of weeks, it's dentistry. Hell, you see it—all of them have rotten teeth, I mean if they have any at all. Besides, it's single-visit care. Itinerant surgery at its best. Pull the tooth, give them some penicillin for a day or two, and they're cured. Believe me, it's one of the few things we can do that might make a difference out here."

"And how do we do it?" Tom asked warily.

David opened his surgical kit and held up two cellophane bags; one contained a small pliers and the other a surgical clamp. "I sterilized them last night in the hospital pressurizer. Got the idea last week."

Tom took the kit and pulled out a small vial.

"Topical thrombin," David said, "to put on the gums to stop any bleeding. Plunkett had an article on its use. Looks real simple—just sprinkle it on the gums and press down for a minute or two. Don't worry," he added, "I promise we won't branch out into brain surgery."

They pulled their first tooth the next day. It took

some coaxing to get the villager, an old man, into the jeep, but the extraction was an unqualified success. The peasants, forgetting their usual sense of caution, crowded around them. The villager sat in the front seat while Tom held his head, and David, standing over him with one leg braced against the dash, the other against the seat, worked the pliers back and forth until the tooth, miraculously intact, came loose. David, triumphant, held up the tooth to a round of spontaneous applause. He winked at Tom.

"I think we're gonna be famous," he said.

David gave the tooth to the old man, who, standing in the jeep, proudly raised it above his head to renewed applause.

They pulled two more teeth that day. The results were equally spectacular. When they left, the villagers stood in the road and waved good-bye. David was ecstatic.

"Not much different from people in the States, huh? All they want is what anyone else wants—results," he said.

Tom was silent, but David, flushed with success, was too happy to notice. Against all odds, they'd been able to do something worthwhile and they'd done it without anyone's help or direction. It was so obvious, he wondered why he hadn't thought of taking care of their teeth before.

"What happens if someone dies?"

"What?"

"No, I mean it," Tom said. "Say one of them villager's a bleeder. Somethin' wrong with his clottin' system, one of those factors like fibrin is down and we don't know it."

"Fibrin," David said. "Where did you hear about that?"

"You mentioned it one of those days when you were talkin' about bleeding problems. I did some checkin', that's all. Now what happens if we pull a tooth, leave, and an hour later they begin to bleed to death?"

"Out here," David said, "the chance of that happening is pretty slim. This isn't exactly the easy life, you know. Anyone with a significant clotting disorder wouldn't last much past infancy, let alone childhood. Don't worry. There aren't going to be any hemophiliacs walking up to the jeep. Come on. Now what's really bothering you?"

"Well," Tom said, "the VC could play up a death, any death. I mean, even if it wasn't our fault. It would only have to look like it was. The VC could use it to get the villagers to set us up. I ain't sayin' they will, but if we get too good—real good at what we're doin'—we could become important, and that ain't so smart—not out here. Ever hear of being targeted?"

David waited.

"It's the kind of thing that happens during firefights when people notice you. Most enemy contacts are a mess—shells going off all over the place, rounds skippin' and whistlin' by, no one knowing what's happenin', people runnin' in all directions, a lot of screamin' and yellin', cries for medics. All kinds of noise. If you get hit, that's it, kind of bad luck. Sometimes, though, in the middle of all the confusion, you know someone's shootin' at you. Not just in your direction, but at you." He glanced over at David. Suddenly he looked older. "Someone sees you. In all that mess, somebody's picked you out. Maybe it was the way you

moved, stood up when someone near you dropped. It
don't matter, though," he said softly. "All that counts is
that someone's seen you. When that happens, you've
got to know it because he's gonna kill you if you don't
kill him first."

"And you think something like that could happen to
us?"

Tom's expression softened. He shrugged. "Hard to
know. Things can change real quick over here."

"No way of getting it to work the other way?"

"The gooks protect us?" He shook his head. "Nah.
These people know that we come and go, but the VC
and North Vietnamese are gonna be here for a long
time. It ain't in their interest to help us. They put up
with us, take what they can, but sooner or later it's their
own they're gonna have to live with. In the Delta, if the
VC didn't get what they wanted from a village, they'd
go in and cut the throats of the village chief's wife and
kids, wire the bodies to the gates. The villagers would
have to push them aside to get in and out. If anyone
cut 'em down before they rotted off the wire, the VC'd
come back, kill someone else, and hang 'em up.
Compared to stuff like that, pullin' teeth don't
carry much weight . . . I ain't sayin' we should stop,"
he added as if anticipating an argument, "just be more
careful."

Tyler was in a snit. He'd walked out of the dispensary
three times, only to return each time more annoyed and
agitated than before. Finally, after checking the desks
and treatment rooms a fourth time, he turned to David.

"Do you know where the hell the Stedman's is? I
can't find it anywhere."

"The medical dictionary? No," David said, "I haven't seen it either."

"Damn it. It's got to be somewhere." He left again, slamming the door behind him.

"You haven't seen it?" Plunkett asked from across the room. He was sitting at the laboratory bench, using the specific gravity meter to check a urine sample.

"No. Why, should I have?"

"Wondering, that's all."

"What's that supposed to mean?"

"I just thought you'd have seen it. Griffen's been borrowing textbooks; I imagine he took the Stedman's."

"Tom?"

"Couple of weeks ago I was looking for Harrison's *Textbook of Medicine*—needed to look up something about pemphigus—and couldn't find it. I asked Sergeant Bradford and he told me that Griffen comes into the dispensary couple nights a week, takes a few textbooks and brings them back before breakfast. He must have forgotten to bring back the Stedman's—or decided that we were too smart to need a medical dictionary."

David shook his head. "And I thought I was such a great teacher. No wonder he's always asked so many questions about things days after we'd discussed them." David smiled. "And fibrin," he said, amused. "Damn. I'm surprised he didn't want to know about factor eight and thromboplastin."

"You didn't tell him to take the books?"

"No, I didn't. I should have," David said, "but I didn't."

Chapter 23

David waited until they had stopped for lunch. "I've been wondering," he said. "Any plans for when you get out?"

"Plans? You mean after the Army?"

"Gonna be a rifleman all your life?"

"What are you talkin' about?"

"The future. And none of that let's-wait-till-the-end stuff."

"Construction, I guess; somethin' like that."

"Where?"

Tom gave David his annoyed but indulgent look. "Atlanta, someplace like that."

"Any money?"

Tom raised an eyebrow. "What about money?"

"You'll need money."

"I've put all my salary into the ten percent overseas soldiers' fund. It'll be enough to get me a car and keep me goin' for a while. What you gettin' at?"

"It doesn't sound like much of a life for someone who's reading medical textbooks in his spare time."

"Oh, that," Tom said under his breath. "I just kind of scan 'em, that's all."

"Oh, I see. I suppose you're into scanning the medical dictionary, too. Take much science in school?"

"A little."

"How did you do?"

"Okay."

"Just okay?"

"Okay," Tom answered sharply.

"And your other classes?"

"What's going on here?" Tom asked, annoyed.

"How did you do?" David asked again.

Tom continued to eat. "Depended," he said.

"Depended? On what? You'll have to get more specific. Colleges like to know things like that."

Tom stopped chewing, his mouth still full. "Colleges?"

"Anyone in your family ever go to college?"

"*My* family?" he blurted, almost choking.

"There must be a university near your home," David said matter-of-factly. "What do you have down there, Georgia State?"

Tom stared at him.

"If you can read medical textbooks, you can read anything. Cramer thinks the Army's a land of opportunity. He might be right. You do have the GI Bill."

Tom went back to his lunch. "You're crazy," he said, dismissing David's comments.

"No," David said, "I'm not, and you know it; and if there's one thing I know about, it's college. It's not any harder than this. Besides, you don't think the people in Georgia aren't going to keep needing doctors?"

"Doctors!" Tom suddenly caught himself and with an indulgent sigh went back to finishing his tin of biscuits.

"It's all right," David said lightly. "New ideas are like the heat over here; they take some getting used to." He left it at that.

Ten minutes later, two helicopters appeared on the horizon, changed directions and flew directly at them. When they were about a quarter-mile away, the gun-ships dropped to ground level. The door gunners waved as they roared past.

"Checkin' us out," Tom said.

Chapter 24

"What do you mean he's gone?" David demanded.

"Cramer sent him back," Tyler said. "It must have been the IV fluids; he woke up this morning after you left. Cramer saw him, talked to him twice—once before and once after lunch—decided the kid was okay and sent him back on the afternoon supply chopper. It won't help to get mad."

"Okay . . . all right," David said angrily. "How did he look?"

"Tired, but okay."

"The kid would have had a better chance if they'd evaced him to a circus instead of here. There's about as much chance of telling if someone's crazy by looking at him and talking for a couple of minutes on a carnival midway as there is after he wakes up from a couple of grams of Thorazine."

"Well, at best, even a psychiatric ward is a tough assessment," Tyler said with unexpected defensiveness.

"Oh, really," David answered. "And Cramer goes home in two days, while he sends this kid who may be seeing his dead friend again this evening back to get his head shot off."

"Cramer's not a bad man. It's like he's a manager of a big steel company. If you told him his plants were polluting the air and water, he'd answer that his job was making steel. I don't know if that makes him evil."

"Just stupid, huh," David said.

"The trooper looked all right," Tyler said again.

"That must have been real comforting to the kid; it sure as hell's going to be comforting to his unit commander. Don't want any crazy-looking kids stepping off the choppers."

"Something bothering you?" Tyler asked.

David ignored the question and poured himself a glass of water out of the ice chest.

"You started to meet with our commander yet?"

"Yeah," Tyler answered, "yesterday. We've begun going over lists. The man is determined not to lose a single paper clip during the transition period."

"And the new colonel?"

"The rank may have been a little inflated. Thorpe tells me the chance of Cramer's replacement being a full colonel or even a lieutenant colonel is remarkably small. We are not, as you are probably aware, a major installation."

David hesitated and then looked at Tyler as if for the first time. "So you may stay commander." There was an embarrassed silence. "You like this, don't you?" David said.

"Parts," Tyler answered with reticence.

"You're thinking of staying in." As soon as he said it, David knew he was right.

"Well," Tyler said, "even if we do understand the Cramers of this world, we can't turn the whole thing over to them, can we?"

"You'll do fine," David said.

Tyler relaxed. "Well, someone's got to do it."

"It couldn't be anyone better."

"Thanks," Tyler said. He actually looked taller, or maybe, David thought, he was only standing straighter. "It means a great deal to me that you think that."

Chapter 25

Cramer left right on schedule. They had a small party in the dispensary. The hospital personnel and the base officers and NCOs were there. Thorpe made a speech of appreciation and presented Cramer with a mounted certificate of merit from both med command and MACV. Cramer, to David's amazement, was pleased with the award and, indeed, touched by what had to be the standard going home plaque. There were the expected reminiscences, but with most of the people Cramer had known during his year already gone, the "good old days" took on a historical rather than a sentimental tone, the people at the party politely listening to stories that mattered to no one but Cramer.

David was struck with the realization that there was no past to Vietnam, no real record of what happened other than what each person carried with him. No two people felt the same way because no two people shared the same experiences. Even those who worked together came at different times and left alone. What affected one man might remain forever unknown to his neighbor. Tyler was right. This was not a five-year war but a one-year war five times.

Cramer ended the party saying something about a reunion. It would never happen, but it was as good a way to end as any.

The next morning, they were all there to say good-bye. Thorpe, Plunkett, Brown, Tyler, Parker, Bradford, the corpsmen and David. Plunkett and Brown helped carry Cramer's gear out to the helipad. When they came back, Plunkett told David there had been tears in Cramer's eyes.

Chapter 26

Nothing unusual happened on the flats for the next ten days; and so with all the villages directly west of the 40th already covered, they moved a little further north into foothills. It was cooler in the hills. Not much cooler, but enough for David to notice the difference.

"It happens like this," Tom said. "It'll be rainin' in a couple of weeks."

"You mean it's actually gonna keep getting cooler?"

"Depends. During the day the edge will be off the heat; the nights, though, especially if you're wet, can get cold."

The first village was over a kilometer from the main road, set back in a natural cul-de-sac.

"Hard to see this one even from the air," Tom said as they parked the jeep.

They had examined more than half the villagers when an old woman, walking up to the jeep, opened her mouth and pointed to a single yellow, rotten tooth.

"Well, what do you know," David said. "We are finally becoming known."

Instead of motioning her to move closer, Tom put

down his stethoscope and looked down the line at the rest of the villagers and then up at the surrounding hills.

"Be back," he said, picking up his rifle and setting off at a jog, jumping over the rocks and small boulders. He didn't slacken his pace until he reached the top of a nearby rise.

David had the woman wait at the side of the jeep and finished up with two more patients before Tom came back down the slope.

"Where you been?" David asked.

"Checkin' to see if there's any roads or paths comin' down out of the hills above this place." Tom put the rifle down, leaning it against the side of the jeep. "There's a path. Not much of one, but walkable, on the other side of the rise. It follows a creek bed that looks like it comes straight out of the hills, and I think, from the size of it, that it gets a lot wider further up." He looked at the woman. "We ain't been here before. Someone had to tell her we pull teeth. There are footprints about two hundred meters up the creek along a gully. Maybe it was just someone from another village, but these people don't travel much. Most spend their whole life in one place. They don't know what's going on in the next valley, much less around the next bend. It's still a little wet up there. Whoever they were, they made sure they crossed over above the village. It must have been at night or they'd have seen the mud. They were carrying some heavy gear, too, and they were keepin' to a good pace."

"So you think they might have been using the creek to come down out of the mountains."

"Why cross above the village, unless they wanted to scout it first? It would have been a hell of a lot easier to use the roads."

"And traveling at night, too," David said.

Tom gestured for the woman to move closer. "Yeah, but the real question is where are they now."

Chapter 27

Tyler had become more talkative, particularly at breakfast. He was taking the job of hospital commander seriously, which surprised Thorpe, and he was enjoying it, which amazed everyone else. Unlike Cramer, he made no pronouncements, but he did stop the daily afternoon meetings at headquarters and set about in a quiet, efficient way to change the call schedules, update the emergency gear and rearrange the triage and mass casualty procedures that had been in place when the 40th was larger. He even added a short evening sick call so that morning call wouldn't need two physicians, freeing the second in case of an emergency.

At first, Thorpe had been suspicious of the changes, but Tyler simply went on as if what he was doing were routine. He even went so far as to ignore Thorpe's coolness, on many occasions passing up the opportunity to make a cynical remark.

The truth was that even though they did little at the 40th, the things they did began to run more smoothly.

They all finished eating at about the same time.

When David got up to leave, Tyler did, too, and they walked outside together. "There's something I think you should know," Tyler said.

"You're going to institute morning formations," David said.

"No, not quite yet," Tyler said. "I was going through the personnel and duty rosters last night. I've got some news you may not like." David waited. "There's no easy way to give this to you. Griffen's extended."

"He what!"

"Sorry. Cramer never mentioned it to me. I only ran across it yesterday, and that was by chance. I found a carbon of the orders."

David was shocked. "You sure?"

"I'm sure."

It took David a moment to collect his thoughts. "When did he do it? No, you don't have to tell me. I already know. It was after I tried to go back out to the village by myself. Damn! How long did he do it for? Never mind. I can figure that out, too . . . Jesus Christ!"

"You can extend three months at a time," Tyler said.

"But he did it for nine, right? The exact amount of time I have left." Tyler nodded. "And that son-of-a-bitch Cramer let him do it."

"Like I said, Ted believes in the war."

"Believed!" David corrected. "He's gone."

"Thorpe agreed to it, too."

"I bet. Probably looks good on his record to have someone from his unit extend for extra duty in this godforsaken desert."

Tyler had enough sense to keep quiet.

David let out a deep, exasperated sigh. "How much longer did he have?"

"You're not going to like it any more than the rest."

"How long?" David demanded.

"Two weeks."

"Two weeks! My God, you mean he could have been home by now."

"No one made him do it."

"Now you are sounding like Cramer."

"He extended because he wanted to."

"You're kidding. He's been out in the boonies so long, he thinks this is the way things are."

"Don't sell him short."

"Sell him short? Christ. It's not that he *could* be home, it's that he *should* be home, and you know it." David managed to get control of himself. "Any way to change it?" he asked.

"No."

"Crazy damn kid . . . nine months." David was furious with himself, Cramer, the Army and Tom. "He never mentioned it."

"Leave it alone," Tyler offered.

"He was worried about me not knowing what the hell I was doing."

"It will be okay," Tyler said. "David"—Tyler hesitated a moment—"you're a lucky fellow."

In the afternoon a gunship flew into the 40th. David was in the dispensary when Sergeant Parker and the crew chief, a lieutenant, walked in.

"The lieutenant wants to know if we can spare some morphine."

"Sure." David went to the medicine cabinet and opened the glass door. "There's a box of forty vials in there. We can get more over in the pharmacy."

"No, sir, I think the forty will do."

David carried the box back to the desk. "Anything going on?"

"No, sir, nothing big, but a lot of little stuff."

"Little stuff . . ."

"Well, sir, hard to tell exactly what's happening. Units are making contact out in the middle of nowhere and the gooks are standing and slugging it out. It's not only in the mountains north of here but all over Nam. Most of the time there's nothing around worth fighting for. Up in I Corps there are a couple of NVA divisions fighting the Marines for three hills near Khe Sanh, and from what we've been told, all those hills protect are another bunch of hills that ain't worth anything. That one's getting to be a big damn battle, tying up half of the tac air in Nam. There must be a couple hundred sorties a day, not to count all the B-52 raids. There's a couple of battles like Khe Sanh only not as big down in the Delta, again over nothing."

"Anything around here?"

"Around here? No, sir, the whole plateau's quiet."

"And in the hills northwest of here? Anyone reporting anything?"

Parker, with a sudden look of concern, stared at David.

"No, sir, nothing."

The next morning, as David walked into the motor pool, Tom stepped back from the jeep like a painter admiring his canvas. A six-foot whip antenna stuck up from the rear bumper.

"Looks good, huh," he said as David walked over to him. "From five meters everyone'd think we had all the air support in Nam at our fingertips."

"Real fine." Tom, excited, didn't notice David's soberness.

"Looks real, too, don't it?"

"Yeah," David answered.

Tom smiled proudly. "Hell, it should. Took it off a real radio. Come on," he said cheerfully, "let's treat the natives."

Tom remained cheerful throughout the rest of the day. David had never seen him so at ease. For the first time since they'd met, he looked actually happy. David didn't say much, but Tom's cheerfulness was infectious, so that by midmorning he found, though he wouldn't have admitted it, that despite his shock and growing embarrassment at Tom's having done so impulsive and stupid a thing as extending, his misgivings began to fade and he started to relax.

"I should have thought of the antenna before," Tom said after they left the second village. "Damn good idea. No one likes to screw around with air strikes."

David agreed it was a good idea. He watched at the next village as Tom examined the villagers, smiling at a few, even letting an old woman listen to her own chest. Maybe Tyler was right, David thought. Maybe it would work out. Occasionally, though, David found himself looking over at the jeep, at the antenna sticking up from the frame. He had forgotten how terribly alone they really were.

Chapter 28

David waited till they were done with the day's work before he brought up the issue of Tom's extending his tour.

"I learned something about the Army yesterday," David said as they were packing up. "You don't have to go back to the States to extend; you can do it right here. You don't even have to go to Saigon."

Tom continued to put the pills in the cartons.

"You extended for nine months."

"I wasn't ready to go home," Tom answered. "Besides, I didn't lose all that much. I still would have had six months left before discharge anyway."

"No difference between six and nine months, huh?"

"I'd rather stay here than do garrison duty with a bunch of lifers somewhere in the States. Besides, lots of people extend."

"I'm not talking about lots of people."

Tom didn't reply.

"Well, at least it gives us time to get things done . . ." Tom, suspicious, stopped filling the cartons. "College," David said. "Think of it as just another prolonged extension of one's tour of duty. Four years instead of nine months. It's settled. I mean it. I'll come and get you after dinner and we'll send out the letters. That's final." Tom saw the look on David's face and didn't argue.

After mess David tracked Tom down in what passed for the NCO club, a small supply building that had been cleaned and partitioned into a small bar and a larger area with half a dozen tables and a 1950s-type jukebox.

"Come on," David said. "There's no one at the dispensary."

"You're serious," Tom said.

"I've never been more serious. You're not afraid, are you?"

Tom looked at the two other troopers in the room, slowly stood and followed David out of the building.

They shut the blackout screens and David turned on the lights in the doctors' area. He pulled two chairs over to what used to be Cramer's desk and turned on the lamp above it. The cone of yellow light diffused gently throughout the dispensary. In its soft glow the green walls and wooden ceiling lost their worn, makeshift look as the dispensary seemed to fold itself protectively around them. Half-hidden in the shadows, the enameled cabinets with their glass doors and rows of shelves filled with beakers and flasks spoke of an earlier, more contemplative time in medicine, a time of penicillin shots and quiet consultations.

Tom, too, was affected by the coziness of the room. As they sat there, the silence mixing with the smells of alcohol and ether, David could see him relax.

"You've been here before at night, haven't you?"

David said. In the dim light Tom's features had softened. David realized how much older he looked than
he really was.

"A few times," Tom answered. "It's quiet here, no
stereos. Nice place to think; kind of comforting."

"Yeah, I like it, too," David admitted. "I didn't think
it was all that much at first, but I do now . . . You didn't
tell Thorpe about the footprints in the creek bed, did
you?"

Tom shook his head.

"I didn't tell Tyler either. If they cancel the med caps,
you could be reassigned, right?" David said. "And with
your skills they wouldn't think twice about another
combat unit."

"That ain't likely to happen."

"No," David answered. "Not while Thorpe and the
computer say you're assigned to med caps at the 40th.
Looks like we're in business for another nine months."

David opened the desk drawer and took out some
paper and envelopes. Across the top of each sheet
gold letters read U.S. ARMY, DEMOCRATIC REPUBLIC OF
VIETNAM; watermarked with the shield of the U.S.
Army.

"Got to admit," David said, holding up the paper, "it's
impressive stationery. Nothing too good for the Army."

Tom didn't smile.

"What's bothering you?" David asked.

Tom looked at the paper for a few moments and then
at David. He didn't look distressed or nervous. He was
serious, though. "I ain't so sure about school." It wasn't
a frivolous comment. "You said you'd been in college
twelve years. That's a long time."

"You take it a year at a time."

"It's more than just the time," Tom said.

"You're not worried about those city boys, are you?"

"Truth is my mother'd worry I'd be oversteppin' myself. Oh, I guess I could learn to live with that. But I've got to think about all that time you put in and what happens if it don't work out. Gotta be tough on anyone, put four, eight, ten years into somethin' before you can use it and then find out it ain't for you, and have nothin' to show for it. I mean, you can't be a lawyer or doctor till you're done with the whole thing. There ain't no half-trained surgeons in the world. I'm right, ain't I?"

"Listen, Tom," David said. "You won't have any trouble. Besides, I don't know about lawyers, but I've never heard of anyone who started medical school who didn't finish."

"No one?" Tom said, surprised. "Must be some damn smart people; I mean, for all of 'em to finish."

David thought for a moment. "You know," he said, "you might just have solved something that's bothered me since I was pre-med. I always wondered where the lousy doctors I'd met had come from. No, I'm not kidding. You're right. You can't be a doctor till you're done, and I'm sure that after three, four, five years, a lot of people are reluctant to say what they've been doing isn't for them. And probably more important, after all that time no one's going to want to fail them." David waited. "Something else is bothering you."

Tom sighed. "Yeah, but I don't know if it's all that important." He hesitated a moment. "Well, I like using my hands, doing things. Been that way since I was a kid."

"College isn't all sitting around and reading. Anyway, who knows—you may even find that you like that part; you like dictionaries, don't you?"

Tom laughed. "Well, I ain't sayin' I don't want to go to college or be a doctor, but . . ."

David raised an eyebrow. "Look. There'll be some tough moments, maybe a lot of them. It's like anything else that's worthwhile. But this isn't all just for you. We could really use a few more doctors who like using their hands."

They wrote four letters, one to the University of Georgia requesting an application to their undergraduate school for the next academic year, a second to Tom's high school requesting a transcript of his records and two more to teachers Tom was sure had liked him, asking for letters of recommendation. There were colleges closer to Tom's home, but Tom admitted as they were talking about schools that one summer his seventh-grade class had traveled to the university and he'd walked around the campus awed by the manicured lawns and the stately buildings.

Tom wavered only once, when he had to sign the letter asking for the transfer of his records.

"I didn't do well in science," he said as if he were confessing.

"Bored?" David asked.

"Sort of," Tom mumbled.

David took his hand and put the pen in it. "Go on, sign. You're not going to be bored anymore."

"I don't know," Tom admitted. "I wish I was writin' away for a huntin' license. I'm a damn good shot."

Chapter 29

David never discussed the med caps with anyone anymore, not even with Tyler, except to say that everything was fine. He didn't want any rumors that things were not going well. He and Tom didn't even talk about them unless they were alone. They continued to go out every other day but stayed on the perimeter of the flats, occasionally working a village in the foothills.

They started to sew up the occasional cut and pack superficial wounds, adding some minor surgery to the tooth extractions. David showed Tom how to put in sutures, and the two of them now discussed surgical as well as medical problems during their lunches, but always with the emphasis on what they could do with their limited resources that would still make sense for the patient and not leave things worse than they found them.

"We can't open any cavity, chest or abdomen," David said. "That's for sure. But we can pack wounds, even deep ones, if we come back within four or five days to remove the packs."

"And drains?" Tom asked.

"Same problem. You've got to be sure you come back and take them out. A foreign body in a wound only makes things worse. There's no chance then of clearing up the infection. It's the reason you pack open wounds of more than eighteen hours instead of just suturing them closed. After half a day, the chance of an open wound getting contaminated is so great that closing it up will lead to an abscess. So you pack them, keeping the wounds open so that they can heal from the bottom and letting any infection drain out the top; sooner or later, though, you've got to remove the pack or the drain."

"Did you learn that in medical school or after?"

David looked up with interest. They had talked very little about school since they'd mailed the letters. David had sensed that Tom wanted it that way.

"After, I guess. I'm sure," David said, thinking for a moment, "that we must have learned the differences between primary and secondary closures of wounds during medical school, but I really only understood it when I was an intern rotating through the emergency room."

"That would have been"—Tom was counting—"at your tenth year. I mean, not counting high school."

"Ninth," David corrected. "But like I said, you take it a year at a time."

Tom looked at the road and the miles of plateau beyond it. "Nine years of schoolin' seems like a lot for what we're doin'."

"We're not doing much; like I said before, this is baseline medicine. All the years of medical school, internship and residency are to be sure that you can handle everything.

"Hell," Tom said, not the least bit impressed, "our doctors at home don't do much more than we do."

"Some patients need more care; subspecialty training takes even longer. Immunology requires a three-year fellowship after a full residency in internal medicine, and neurosurgery is at least another six or seven after you finish your general surgery training."

"I don't know," Tom said. "We ain't seen no brain tumors and I don't remember any at home either. Most people there have infections, anemia, stuff like that, just like the people out here. Couple years should be all you need to help 'em."

"Tom," David said appreciatively, "you're going to be a very challenging student."

A few days later they were on a narrow dike across a dry creek bed barely wide enough for the jeep. Both of them had to lean over the sides and watch the wheels to keep from going over the edge. Tom was moving the jeep forward a few feet at a time when, at the opposite end of the dike, a group of Vietnamese suddenly appeared. The first two had stepped onto the causeway before they saw the jeep. When they finally did see it, they stopped so quickly that those behind bumped into them. David, the wheels on his side clear of the edge, looked up and saw them first.

The Vietnamese stood like statues. There were seven of them. David reached over and touched Tom's leg.

"What is it?" Tom mumbled, still leaning over the side, watching the left side of the jeep. As he turned, he saw the Vietnamese. "Don't move," he whispered, still bent over. He reached under the dash and, pulling the rifle over to him, sat up and put both hands on the top of the wheel.

There was a small ledge near the end of the dike. As the jeep moved closer to the Vietnamese, the first two stepped onto the ledge while the others moved to the end of the dike.

Tom, acting as if nothing was wrong, continued to glance down at the tires, but he kept his hands visible, on top of the wheel. There wasn't a sound. Whatever the Vietnamese's initial confusion, it had been replaced by stony silence.

The jeep rolled past the first two, missing them by inches, but neither moved. David could feel the hostility. The others weren't going to get out of the way either. As the jeep edged past the next two, David's arm brushed one of their knapsacks. He could feel something hard, like a shell or grenade.

A strange discipline held them all, as if they each knew that as long as no one moved everyone would be okay.

Tom kept the jeep rolling forward. The last three Vietnamese stood like pillars, their square faces completely expressionless. David realized he had not drawn a breath since they'd seen the Vietnamese. They finally cleared the end of the causeway. David didn't dare turn around. "I know," Tom said under his breath, "something's wrong."

As soon as they were out of sight of the Vietnamese, Tom pressed down on the accelerator and, taking the jeep off the road, drove it a hundred yards across the open ground to the foot of the nearest hill.

Leaving the motor running, he grabbed the M-16.

"Get the binoculars," he said. They scrambled up the slope together, crawling the last few yards to the crest.

"Those weren't refugees," David said.

The seven Vietnamese had continued on across the causeway and stopped on the other side of the dike. They seemed to be arguing. Tom took the binoculars from David, kept them on the Vietnamese for two or three minutes and then, searching the hills on both sides of the causeway, found something.

"Over there at nine o'clock behind that ridge," he said, handing David the lenses.

David adjusted the focus and a small, paved road came into view.

"That's the road they should be on."

David swung the binoculars back to the Vietnamese. The two who had led the group had fallen in behind the others. They were talking as they walked along, occasionally looking back over their shoulders in the direction of the causeway. There was something familiar about those two, about all of them.

"They're VC, aren't they?" David asked.

"No." Tom took back the binoculars. "That ain't the way VC walk, not when they don't think anyone's watchin'. They like to gossip. These walk single file. They're used to walkin' that way, and they ain't screwin' around. Did you notice how sweaty they were? They've been doing some movin'. And they were real surprised to see us. If they were from around here they'd be used to seeing GIs or at least, with all the ARVNs, U.S. jeeps."

"There was something in one of the knapsacks," David said. "Felt like a grenade."

"Yeah," Tom said. "Well, one thing's for sure. They ain't refugees. Come on. Let's get back to the jeep."

They crawled back off the slope together, and when they were clear of the rise, stood up.

"NVA?" David asked.

"In civilian clothes? Not likely."

"North Vietnamese cadre then," David said, "sent down to work with the VC."

"If they were cadre, they wouldn't be movin' during the day, not by themselves anyway. They'd be movin' with VC who'd be showin' 'em the way. They wouldn't want to be on their own this far south."

"Then who are they?"

"Don't know."

David couldn't shake the feeling that he'd seen them before. "I guess we'd better tell Thorpe," he said.

"You sure?" Tom asked. "What are you gonna tell him? This is still an officially secure area, and there ain't been no trouble for months. Lifers don't like being told secure areas ain't secure. Besides, if they are NVA, where are their weapons? We ain't the only troops movin' around out on these flats. We got choppers flyin' over this area all the time and there's a lot of ARVNs around. If them gooks do have their weapons in those knapsacks, they wouldn't stand a chance. You saw what happened back there. If we'd been an ARVN unit, they'd be dead now. NVA are too professional for that. I'll tell you this much," Tom said, "it don't make sense."

David shook his head. "I can't help feeling I've seen them before." But he didn't say it very loudly.

* * *

David didn't tell anyone what had happened. Tom was right; there was nothing to tell. The first question was bound to be "Are you sure?" You needed facts, whether it was medicine or the Army. Besides, why jeopardize the med caps. No sense making trouble where there might not be any.

After dinner David took his usual evening walk, but the feeling he'd had on the hill kept intruding. He could not shake the sense that he had seen those Vietnamese before. He stopped at the helipad, and as he turned to leave he found himself staring at the communications building diagonally across from him. He quickly turned and looked back at the pad. There was a sudden flash of recognition. "Of course," he said and hurried up the path.

Tom was in the barracks. "Come outside," David said. They walked until they were well clear of the building. "Those weren't regular NVA today," David said. "They were assault troops, shock troops, whatever you want to call them. I told you this afternoon there was something familiar about them. It's been bothering me ever since. Then a few minutes ago out at the helipad, I figured it out. It was the look on their faces. It was the same look as those assault troops from the 25th, the ones you thought you knew. They moved the same way, too. Those were hard-core soldiers we saw today. They didn't expect us, but they didn't do anything stupid either, and they weren't afraid. They saw the antenna and they stood still. No one panicked. I think there's more of them, too. Remember the cloth on the rock, those footprints along the creek bed the other day, and the shirt in the hamper? You were right.

Weapons or not, there's something going on around here."

"All right," Tom said without hesitation. "We've got a day before we got to go out again. Let me think about it. I'll see you tomorrow after breakfast."

David knew he was right, but he still didn't quite believe that he and Tom had discovered something a whole army had missed. The chopper pilot he'd given the morphine to had said there was nothing going on around the 40th, and nothing had been reported.

Tom came to the dispensary a little before ten. "No one here?"

"No, just me."

For the first time in weeks Tom looked ill at ease. "I've been thinkin' about all this," he said. "Somethin' is happenin', but I don't know what. You get feelin's about things over here, a kind of sixth sense, but you can lose it real quick. Maybe it's bein' out of the real heavy stuff. It's the reason a lot of guys pass up their R and Rs. There were a couple weeks down in the Delta when I was attached to a company of the Riverines. One of their patrols got ambushed and all of 'em—ten or eleven—were wasted. Claymore went off. It had to have been command detonated to have gotten 'em all. I found the wire and followed it back to within twenty-five meters of a small village. At night, I went into the village with two or three of 'em. First two huts I went into standin' up. At the third one I stopped. Can't tell you why. All of a sudden, it was like I knew I was doing somethin' wrong. There wasn't much of a moon, but enough, if you looked close, to pick objects out of the shadows. I went into the third hut on my belly. Soon as I pushed open the door, the whole top half got blown away. I saw the muzzle blast and killed the gook. He must have been watching me, seen me go into the other two huts standin' up, figured I'd do the same thing again." Tom looked worried. "I should have been able to figure out who they were," he said dejectedly, "but I didn't, and I can't figure out what shock troops would be doin' dressin' up like refugees, and without weapons, or weapons they couldn't get at. It don't make any sense. Maybe we should stop."

"But nothing's happened," David said. "They didn't want trouble any more than we did. Listen, we're still safer out here than anywhere else. We'll stay out of the hills from now on, close to the 40th. Okay? Agreed?"

"Agreed."

They did stay near the 40th, sometimes visiting the same village twice in a week. David simply continued to file the regular reports, writing in the names of villages they should have visited. They met no more groups of refugees, nor did they see any more footprints. Still, David was anxious. He was not as worried about himself and Tom as he was about the 40th. Tom had been sure that no one would listen and David shared his feelings, but there was the nagging thought that even if he and Tom were not personally at any greater risk than usual, the 40th might be. For days he debated whether he should tell someone.

But who would believe that anyone was going after the 40th? For the little that he and Tom did, the 40th did even less. So David, balancing the benefits against

the risks, always drifted back to keeping silent. If he
and Tom had found anything more to make them suspicious, he'd have said something, but they hadn't. And
nothing happened. Yet the feeling that something was
going on and that someone at the 40th should know
worked on David. Finally, he decided he should at least
tell Lieutenant Brown. Brown, like Thorpe, was regular
Army, and David was sure he could mention it to him
without arousing his suspicion, something he wasn't so
sure he'd be able to do with Thorpe. He didn't want to
jeopardize the med caps even temporarily if there was
no reason.

It was the very fact that nothing else had happened
that ultimately gave him the confidence to talk to
Brown. He waited till the afternoon and walked to the
headquarters building. He told Brown that they'd been
seeing groups of refugees on side roads and passing
through some of the villages.

"Griffen never mentioned anything like that," Brown
said.

"Oh, he didn't think it was worth reporting," David
answered quickly. "I guess I'm a little more nervous
than he is," he added.

Brown grinned. "Yeah," he said appreciatively, "he's
a cool one."

David told Brown about the hut; not about the grenade, only about finding the shirt with the star on it,
and also the footprints that Tom had found above the
village with the woman who'd wanted her tooth pulled.

Brown took it all in. "You haven't seen anything
around here, though, have you?"

"No . . . nothing."

"Well," Brown said, "there's always been some infiltration across the flats, but no one's seen anything recently. If there were big movements, someone would have seen 'em. Don't worry."

"Oh, I'm not really worried," David said. "I just wanted to know what you thought, kind of a second opinion."

"Any time, Doc," the lieutenant said. "Any time."

Relieved, David walked away. Tom was right. No one did want any part of it. Either Brown didn't think what he was told was important, or else he thought what happened away from the 40th wasn't his responsibility. It was Tyler's and Cramer's views of Vietnam all wrapped up together. Everyone doing his own little part and no one watching anyone else. Crazy, David thought, but it did have the advantage of letting you do what you wanted.

Nothing happened for the next two weeks. The flats around the 40th were clear of any movement. They didn't even meet anyone on the roads.

Then one morning on the edge of one of the great basins southwest of the 40th, David and Tom saw another group of refugees. They watched them through their binoculars as they moved across the flats. There were six this time.

"All men again," Tom said, putting down the binoculars. "Come on, let's see where they've been." He drove slowly to keep down the dust. "It's early," he said, "so they've had to make camp somewhere around here. I don't think they'd be travelin' at night, not out here. Look real funny in the middle of nothin' to have someone find you sleeping during the day."

When they reached their tracks, Tom turned the

jeep away from the direction the Vietnamese had taken and backtracked, following the footprints across the basin. They drove for more than an hour.

"Over there," Tom said finally, pointing to a hollow. "That's where they stopped."

He took his rifle and they walked the last twenty yards to where he'd pointed. There wasn't a sound; there was nothing moving for miles.

"No fire. They're eatin' cold rations . . . see." Tom kneeled and ran his hand gently across the ground. There were little pieces of rice mixed with the dirt. "And look here." David kneeled next to him. There was a faint mark on the ground. David could see the cross-hatching. "That's the imprint of the butt of a Siminov attack rifle. They have a kind of serrated pattern on the shoulder stock." He brushed aside a small mound of dirt. "Chewin' tobacco; they aint' even smokin'." He stood and looked around. "See over there, that pile of rocks?" There was a small mound of rocks out in the middle of a level area a short distance from the hollow. It was in clear view of anyone coming in from the west. "This place has been used before. That's a cairn, a trail marker. They can be used as signs, too. If the rocks on the top are knocked off, it can mean stay away; two cairns side by side can mean leave supplies here, things like that. They got to let their own people know what's goin' on." Tom started checking the other directions. "Looks like they're moving in from the west along a line directly below the 40th, most likely skirting it. I'll tell Major Thorpe. Hell, there's probably a pile of rocks every kilometer from here to Saigon."

David looked at the rocks again. "You know, Tom, if they need the cairns, then there's got to be new groups coming through all the time. It means that they are on their own; no one from down here's taking them through. These troops don't know what to expect out here. They probably haven't been this far south before, and there must be a lot of them."

Tom thought for a moment.

"And there's something else," David said. "They're traveling light, so they've got to eat as they move along, and they aren't going into any villages. No one's reported them taking any food. It's all got to be set up for them. There have to be food caches out here."

"Meaning?" Tom said, looking at David.

"Meaning that this is all real organized. There's something big going on somewhere."

They drove out of the basin toward the 40th over a series of great parallel slabs of earth, each a kilometer or two in length. In the rainy season they would be plates of mud.

"Over there." Tom slowed the jeep. Far across the flats they could see figures moving, no more than reeds shimmering in the waves of heat.

David took out the binoculars and focused on the figures. "Five more," he said, "and all men." He turned in his seat, giving the whole plateau a quick scan. "When we get back we'll have Thorpe send out a chopper to check these guys out."

The road ran straight for a half-mile and then turned, disappearing for a short distance into one of the many depressions that crisscrossed the flats. They were half-way to the turn when a metallic sound came from the front of the jeep. A moment later, there was another sharp sound.

"Down!" Tom yelled. He pressed his foot hard on the

gas pedal and the jeep shot forward. David had to grab
the door handle to keep his balance. The air was snapping around them.

"Tom!" But even as he yelled, Tom had slammed on
the brakes, throwing the jeep into a hard right-hand
skid. Four Vietnamese were standing at the dip in the
road.

While the jeep was skidding, Tom slammed his foot
on the gas again and, spinning the wheel, threw the
jeep into a left-hand skid so that it spun around, driver's side facing the turn. Even before the jeep came to
a stop, he'd picked up the M-16 from the floorboard
and in one motion pointed it down the road and emptied the clip. With the roar of the automatic, the first
two Vietnamese fell over and the others leaped for the
ditches. A flash of orange engulfed the road. Tom
pulled out another clip, reloaded and, turning the
wheel, drove straight toward the sprawled figures.

The next instant the ground in front of them lifted
into the air. The jeep careened through the dust and
debris. Behind them a series of explosions went off, one
after the other.

The jeep bounced as it hit the first body. David lost
his balance. There was a second explosion and a great
wall of flame rushed past him. For an instant the air
itself seemed to catch fire, and then the jeep lifted into
the air and David was thrown out. All he remembered
was tumbling free. There had been no time for panic.
He hit something hard and then he was tumbling
again, unable to catch his breath.

It was the light that brought him back to consciousness. The sun was in the wrong place. Confused, David
struggled to hang on to the fact, not to let it go. Every-

thing was backward. The shadows were all going in the wrong direction. He knew it was important to remember why, but he couldn't. It took some time to realize that it wasn't the sun that was turned around but the road. David managed to get to his feet. The acrid smell of explosives stung his nose.

For a second or two he didn't know where he was. He stared uncomprehending at the trail of debris, the cartons and bottles strewn along the side of the road. Then he saw the skid marks. There was a sudden moment of recollection, and with it he felt the pain in his back and shoulder. He hobbled back to where the jeep had gone off the road, and followed the tire tracks till they disappeared in the rocks and hard-packed earth of the plateau. He stopped where the tire tracks ended but couldn't see the jeep.

It was nowhere to be seen, nor was Tom. A feeling of panic began to take hold of him. There was something he knew he should remember, something important. Fighting the panic, David quickly turned again and stared at the road as if for the first time.

He realized the dip in the road shielded them from whoever had set up the ambush. He wiped his face and was surprised to find blood. Oddly, the sight of it suddenly calmed him. Would they come to see what had happened? How much time did he have? Startled, he suddenly remembered the Vietnamese at the turn. The gun! Of course, that was what he was trying to remember. Frantic, he looked around again. Then he saw the spare tire lying on the ground twenty yards from where he stood. Limping, he hurried over. As he neared the tire, he saw the jeep turned over in a gully. The windshield was gone and the paint on its hood was burned black.

As David limped up to the jeep, he saw the M-16 on the ground and quickly picked it up. But the breech was jammed. While he worked at it, he saw Tom lying facedown a few yards away, ahead of the jeep. Shifting the rifle to his good arm, he scrambled over the rocky ground. Tom was breathing, but his head was cut. David reached under Tom's shoulder.

"It's me . . . it's okay," David said, carefully turning him over. The cut was a gash that began above his eye and continued down across the bridge of Tom's nose. It laid open his cheek down to the bone. Blood covered his face.

Tom struggled to sit up.

"No . . . no," David said.

Despite the size of the wound, it was barely bleeding. David quickly felt Tom's arms and legs. There were no fractures.

"Stoppin' for them gooks on the road threw off their aim," Tom said. There was a strange, distant quality to his voice. David helped him get more comfortable. "They had us set up; must have figured we'd seen enough, but stoppin' screwed up their timing." He didn't fight David anymore and let him put his head back on the ground. He coughed, and a tiny bit of reddish foam filled the corner of his mouth. David looked closer at Tom's chest. There were two small holes in his T-shirt. The same red foam was sucked in and out of them with each breath.

"Tom," David said, "I think you're hurt. I'm going to get some bandages and the canteens out of the jeep."

David took the surgical kit from under the dash.
Then he gathered the canteens, but as he stood, he
froze. Two Vietnamese were standing in the middle of
the road. For a blind moment he waited for the sound
of gunfire, but then he saw they had no weapons. A
moment later the road was empty again. Whoever they
were, they had to have seen the jeep. As he turned to
go back to Tom, David realized that Tom had had his
rifle pointed directly at them the whole time.

The blood flowing from the gash on Tom's face was
just a trickle.

David lifted Tom's head and held the canteen to his
lips. "You've got to drink this, Tom. It'll help keep up
your blood volume." He managed to sound matter-of-
fact. Tom took a few sips and turned his head.

"You got hit in the chest," David said. "I don't know
how bad, but I'm going to put a surgical pack over the
wound. It'll help you breathe."

Tom shifted himself sideways so that he could see
the jeep. "Didn't burn, huh?" David tried to get him to
lie back, but Tom refused. "The inside's still okay,"
Tom said. "I mean, the seats and stuff. Nothin' burned
up." He seemed to gather some strength. David started
to open the surgical pack.

"Your shoulder don't look so good."

"What . . ."

"And your nose looks broken."

"They'll mend," David said.

Using the scissors from the surgical kit, he cut off
Tom's T-shirt. The two holes were an inch below his
shoulder. David put the pack over both of them and
taped down the edges. Tom started to breathe easier,

but David couldn't be sure how long the seal would
hold. Tom was looking past him at the road.

"I'm going to have to go and get some help. I want
you to finish the water while I'm gone." He held up the
canteen for another drink, but Tom started to cough
and turned his head away.

"Tom, you're bleeding into your chest. You've got to
drink to keep your blood volume up."

"In the canvas bag." David put the two canteens
down next to him. "In the canvas bag," Tom said again,
"in the back of the jeep. It's got to still be there."

"What does?"

"In the back under the tarp."

David thought Tom might be hallucinating.

"Go on, get it! We ain't got all that much time. Go
on, damn it . . . they may come back." Then he started
to cough again.

Reluctantly David went back to the jeep. He pulled
what boxes and gear were left out of the rear and then
took off the tarp. A canvas bag fell out from under it.
He stared at the bag and then, with a sense of relief so
real that he could feel it wash over him, he tore loose
what remained of the adhesive that held the bag to the
seat. Opening the straps, he slid out the grenade
launcher. There was a shotgun round and grenade
taped to the stock. He quickly loaded the launcher and
looked up at the road again, only this time with confidence.

"Found it?" Tom said. "Been there a long time; put
it there the first day. Remember, you didn't want no
weapon." His voice was almost a whisper. "You know,
I can't see so clear anymore."

"You got that cut on your head. There's blood getting into your eyes, that's why you can't see," David said comfortingly. "It'll be okay."

"Yeah," Tom answered as he wiped his forehead. But when he looked at his hand there was no blood. "Yeah," he said softly. "Must be all the blood."

But David didn't hear. He was beginning to think about what to do. He couldn't be sure who the Vietnamese he saw at the turn were; they looked like the ones who had been on the road right before the mortars hit. They weren't carrying weapons so maybe they were only refugees or villagers using the road. All anyone else on the other side of the depression could know was that the jeep had made the turn and not come out from around the bend. Without seeing what had happened, no one would know if they were okay or not. They wouldn't know if they'd used the radio, whether an air strike or a gunship was already on the way. But if he walked out, whoever had ambushed them would know something was wrong. Of course, there was a possibility that whoever had ambushed them was gone already. They wouldn't want to stay around and be caught in the open by a couple of fighter bombers.

They could wait here, but for what? No one even knew where they were. He'd been filing routes that they weren't taking. It would be getting hotter as it got closer to noon. Tom wouldn't be able to stay out much longer, not in this heat. There wasn't any choice.

"Tom," David said, "I'm going to have to leave."

"Give it to me . . . no," Tom said, waving away the launcher that David handed to him, "the M-16. It's no good; see, the breech is broken. What were you going

to do, throw it at 'em? Come on . . . give it here. Don't
worry," Tom said. "I'll be okay."

David took off his shirt and stretched it across two
rocks to help shade Tom's face and chest.

"Here's the water," David said. He had put the canteens where Tom could reach them. "Drink as much
as you can, a little bit every couple of minutes. I'll be
back as soon as I can."

Tom grabbed his arm. "I should have figured it out,
shouldn't I . . . if them gooks knew what they were
doin', I should have known. It ain't all that hard."
He stifled a cough. "Damn, how the hell did I miss it
all . . ." But it wasn't a question anymore.

"You didn't miss anything," David said. "I did. I'll get
back as soon as I can."

Tom, glancing past him at the road, suddenly looked
very weary. "It's all inches over here. There never was
much margin." David started to say something. "No,"
Tom said, stopping him. "Happens all the time. But it's
not so terrible. The bad thing's when they beat you
when you're at your best. No, I mean it. We was into
somethin' else, fixin' people. Gettin' good at it, too.
Damn hard to do two things real good. You always get
sloppy at one, lose the edge . . ." His voice trailed off.
But he didn't sound disappointed, only tired.

David handed him the M-16.

Tom took the rifle and put it across his lap. "Just
point the launcher in the direction you want to fire; the
shotgun round will blow away anything in front of you
up to fifty meters. Something further, use the grenade
round."

"I'll hurry back."

"Sure . . . Doc?" Tom looked at him, his eyes sharply focused, crystal clear again as they used to be. "You think I could have done it . . . become a doctor?"

"Yeah," David said. "If I was ever sure of anything, I was sure of that."

Tom looked relieved. "Yeah," he said proudly, "I could have done it; college at least . . . huh."

He shifted the rifle so that the trigger was closer to his right hand. "See you when you get back. Better go," he said. "No sense standin' around."

David did not hesitate at the turn. In a world once filled with possibilities, there were now only two. Either the VC or NVA were there, or they weren't. He ran past the bodies of the Vietnamese. A half-mile ahead he saw three figures moving across the flats at right angles to the road. He ran past the shell craters. Nothing happened. Finally he forced himself to slow to a pace he knew he'd be able to sustain. It was no longer a race to be won but a race not to be lost. He looked up at the sun. It was almost directly overhead.

After a quarter-mile the stiffness in his right side subsided to a dull ache, and he was able to increase his pace. The heat that had been such a burden in the past became an asset. It worked on his arm and shoulder, loosening his sore muscles, soothing the pain.

He ran on, the sweat dripping down his neck and back. The flats soon became a blur. He kept running, moving through endless curtains of heat, the only sound his boots pounding on the rock-hard earth. It became a kind of cadence, a drumbeat that was all that mattered. He didn't have to think anymore, he only had to listen.

He'd slow down but the rhythm would push him forward again. The launcher became a counterweight to his injured right side, acting as a kind of pendulum, keeping his balance, dragging him forward. Rocks and shadows shimmering in the distance moved closer and disappeared, only to be replaced by new rocks and newer shadows. There was a moment when he moved so effortlessly that he thought he'd dropped the launcher and was surprised to see it still there, swinging at his side. He ran on past exhaustion, past feeling, back into a world before oxygen, a place where nothing mattered but physics, where all that kept him going was his own momentum.

He tripped and managed to keep his balance. But the effort left him drained. He wanted to stop, to rest, to be able to breathe again. But somehow he was still moving and that seemed all that mattered. How long he ran on like that he never knew.

Slowly, almost imperceptibly, he became aware that something was wrong. He kept running but knew that it was not the same anymore. He managed to lift his head and look around, but nothing had changed. Still, the feeling that something was different kept intruding. It was like a dull but persistent pain that at first could be ignored, but after awhile, never leaving, began to work on you, forcing its way by degrees into your consciousness, until . . . Suddenly with what seemed to be his last bit of energy, he realized it was his footsteps. The sound of his footsteps had changed. They were no longer muffled, distant. The sound was sharper, crisper. It was as if someone else were running. But there wasn't anyone else.

He forced himself to look down. It was the road. David could barely see through the sweat and exhaustion, but the road had changed. He tried to understand. Then it came to him like a revelation. The road was paved! Gasping, his lungs burning, he managed to stop. It took him what seemed like minutes to straighten up. He was on the main road, but which way had he turned?

He'd have to go back to where the two roads met. But where was that? Which way, right or left? He tried to remember, forcing himself to concentrate, fighting the numbness that threatened to overwhelm him. He looked at his watch, barely able to keep his eyes in focus long enough to see the dial. Almost an hour since he'd left Tom. The sense of panic returned. It was a long time. There was something else to remember, something Tom had once said. They had been on the ridge, looking through the binoculars. Of course, David thought. Suddenly he was thinking again. You hitch-hiked on paved roads. There were trucks!

David lifted the launcher and started to run again, though it was really no more than a shuffle. It no longer mattered which way he'd turned. He hobbled and dragged himself along for another twenty minutes before he saw a tiny speck moving across the flats. It vanished and reappeared. David sat on the edge of the asphalt, the launcher between his legs, and waited. He was too exhausted to feel relief.

The truck slowed and came to a stop a few yards in front of him, the motor running. Two soldiers opened the doors and looked around nervously before they climbed out of the cab. The driver stayed close to the truck. The other trooper continued to look around as he crossed to David's side of the road. To stand, David had to use the launcher as a crutch.

"You okay?" the corporal asked, still glancing around cautiously.

"Yeah," David answered. "I'm a doctor at the 40th. My driver and I got hit ten, twenty kilometers from here, down one of the dirt roads. He's still out there." David started to limp toward the truck. "We got to get him." The corporal followed. The driver, a sergeant, didn't move. "The road's about a mile back."

The corporal, uneasy, stopped a few feet behind David. "Well, sir, we don't exactly know what's still out there."

David didn't hesitate. As he turned around, he raised the barrel of the launcher so that it was level with the corporal's midsection. "The road's clean. I just came down it. Now you or your buddy can either come or stay." His finger tightened on the trigger.

It took less than five minutes to reach the turnoff. David sat, eyes closed, resting his chin on the barrel of the launcher. The hot breeze coming in through the open window was all that kept him awake.

He had them slow as they came to the straight stretch of road. The mortar craters ran for a hundred yards right up to the turn. Suddenly he sat bolt upright. "Stop!" Opening the door to the cab, he jumped down. The bodies of the Vietnamese were gone. As he ran, a terrible premonition took hold of him.

He didn't stop at the turn but ran on across the road to where he could see the ground on the other side of the depression. The jeep lay where it had been, but the ground around it had been picked clean. The broken cartons and bottles were gone. David, unmoving, just stood there.

The corporal walked up beside him. "That him there, sir?" They'd stripped his body and left it sprawled on the top of a small slope.

"Bring up the truck." David left the edge of the road and started across the flats to where they'd dragged Tom's body. He should have stayed. Or else he should have checked the road and then come back to give Tom the launcher. But he hadn't.

David slowly stopped walking and stared. "My God," he whispered. They had cut off Tom's ears and nose and hacked off his arms and feet. There was no way of anyone knowing who he was anymore; all that was recognizable was the gash running across what was left of his face. David no longer felt or heard a thing; the heat, his exhaustion, the noise of the truck, his fear. He'd been a fool; yet with a sudden terrible clarity he understood that he'd been sent away, and that from that moment on, no matter what else happened, there would be no way of knowing who had really left the other.

The motor was still running as the sergeant and corporal walked past him. "We'll pick him up, sir," the corporal said.

David continued to stare. He heard nothing. Of course, he thought, Tom had to have known how badly injured he was. He had to have known that without help an hour in this heat would be too long.

David waited until they carried the body past him and then walked over to where he'd left Tom and picked up his shirt, torn and bloody, from the ground.

He left the rifle where it was. A few moments later the corporal came back.

"We've got him loaded, sir." David didn't answer. The trooper hesitated. "Maybe he was dead before they did all that stuff," he said.

"Did you find the rest of him?"

"Well, no, sir," the corporal answered. "We tried but we couldn't." Nervously he glanced back at the driver, who had walked up and stood beside the overturned jeep. "Sir," he said, "it's gettin' late. We should get out of here."

"I'll start with this gully. You two start over near where they left him . . . he liked using . . ."

"Captain!" David felt something hard pushed into his back. "Don't turn around, sir. If you do, I'll kill you."

"Jim, take the launcher." The corporal walked in front of him and took the weapon from David.

"He's dead, sir," the corporal said gently, as if apologizing for the driver. "He ain't gonna know nothin'. You're pretty close to collapsing yourself. Your arm's broken or something and you're all cut up. Besides, it'll be dark in a few hours. Come on," the corporal said. "We got some water in the truck. It don't make no sense to stay out here; you can come back in the morning. If his . . . well, if they're here now, they'll be here tomorrow."

"Tomorrow?" David said, as if surprised to hear the word.

"Jim!" The driver pointed to the west. Two pillars of smoke were rising off the plateau. "Let's get out of here."

"Sir, come on. He's dead. It ain't gonna do you no good to get yourself killed."

Chapter 30

David and the corporal carried the body off the truck. Within minutes Tyler was at the dispensary, Thorpe and Plunkett no more than a few seconds later. David paid no attention to any of them. He put the body into one of the treatment rooms and then walked back outside. A few of the base personnel were standing around the truck. Brown had arrived, and he and Thorpe were talking to the driver. Everyone stopped and stood silently as David walked past them. He opened the truck door and took out the grenade launcher.

Tyler walked over to him. "I'm going to have them take Tom to the morgue. I think we'd better fix you up. Come on, it won't take long."

Plunkett sewed the lacerations on David's face. Tyler had them take X rays of his shoulder. It wasn't broken, but his clavicle was dislocated and two of his ribs had been fractured.

It took a half-hour to finish suturing the cuts and remove the smaller pieces of shrapnel from his chest and shoulders. In the dispensary Tyler supervised the treatment while Thorpe asked questions, careful to stick to the essentials. David answered calmly, precisely, telling Thorpe about the cairns and the groups of Vietnamese he and Tom had met, the booby-trapped hamper, though he hardly heard his own voice.

He was sure that whoever had ambushed them had seen the jeep drive across the flats to the rockpile and then had watched through binoculars when they'd stopped the second time. Tom had been right. They didn't know exactly what they'd found, but someone else was worried that they did.

"The NVA are moving their troops across the plateau," David said in answer to Thorpe's question about why he thought they'd removed the bodies. "Assault troops for sure, and hard-core regulars. That's probably why they went after us. They saw the antenna and thought we had a radio; someone must have figured since we'd already found one of their rest areas and might find more, it was better to take the chance of getting rid of us than run the risk of our finding something else and calling in some choppers. They got rid of the bodies because they didn't want them lying around for anyone else to find. Maybe they were NVA so they buried or hid them."

Thorpe wasn't convinced. "But they let you go," he said.

"Yeah," David said softly, "they let me go."

"If they're going to go to all the trouble of hiding dead bodies, why not go after you, too?"

"Why not," David answered wearily, his own exhaustion protecting him from whatever Thorpe was asking. "I don't know," David said. "Maybe they weren't so sure what to do. They knew they didn't get us. We made it to the turn. They couldn't see us anymore. For all they knew, we'd already called in their position. It was easy to decide to kill us, not so easy to decide what to do when they didn't succeed. When I walked out, they didn't know what the hell was going on. Maybe they thought if they let me go, the Army'd write it off as just a random sniping, something without any purpose, another one of those things. I don't know. They might have pulled out, got around the turn and seen the jeep was a wreck. But who knows? All I do know is that they're still out there."

Plunkett finished taping his shoulder. "Okay," Tyler said, interrupting, "you're done. Why don't you go get some rest. The major will talk to you tomorrow." Thorpe didn't argue.

"When's the body going out?" David was surprised at how calm he sounded.

"Tomorrow," Tyler said. "There's a supply chopper scheduled in around noon."

David climbed off the table. Everything hurt.

"Would you like something to help you sleep?" Tyler asked.

"You mean a little Thorazine and when I wake up everything will be okay?"

"No," Tyler said, "I don't mean that at all, but you could use some sleep."

"I'll lie down, but I got a few things to do first."

Tyler motioned Plunkett to let him go.

The enlisted barracks was almost empty. Most of the troopers were at lunch. The few who were there looked up as he walked in.

Tom's bunk was perfectly made, the blanket pulled tight at the corners. David opened Tom's locker, took out his wallet and a neatly wrapped packet of letters. He was about to close the locker when he saw the dictionary. He stared at it a moment and then reached inside and took it out. There were pieces of paper sticking out from the pages.

The armory was unlocked. David walked down the wooden walkway to the back, where the ammunition was stored. He found the crate stenciled M-79 ammunition, took out two shotgun rounds, put them into his pockets, and then walked back to his own barracks.

Tyler didn't have to tell him how tired he was, but he wanted to get everything done before he collapsed. He put the shells with the letters and wallet in his locker, hid the launcher under the bed, set the alarm and lay down. He fell asleep holding the dictionary.

David didn't dream. One moment he was asleep and the next, with the first sound of the alarm clock, he was awake. It was still dark, but through the edges of the curtains he could see the sky lightening. He got up and managed, despite the pain, to dress and leave the barracks without making any noise. Outside, the heavy morning air swirled the mists that covered the open ground between the buildings.

As David passed the mess hall, Tyler stepped out of the doorway. "No breakfast?" he asked.

"I'm going to gas up a jeep. Then I'll come back and get some coffee."

"Feel strong enough to go back out?"

"I slept okay."

"The med caps have been canceled, David, at least until we find out what's going on."

"I'm not going to visit any villages."

"You look in the mirror this morning? I don't know what you're running on, but whatever it is, there isn't much left."

"I said I feel okay."

"No one knows what's happening out there."

"It'll only be for a couple of hours. I'll be back by noon."

"Sorry, we can't risk it."

"Thirty minutes out there is all I'll need."

"No one's going to let you go out alone, and after yesterday Thorpe's not about to let any personnel off the base. I'm not kidding, David. *Not for any reason!*"

"Look, Herb," David said. "I should have stayed out there and looked. I'm not going to make a big search of it. He came here in one piece. The least we can do is send him home the same way. I want all of him buried together. It isn't a hell of a lot to ask."

"I'm sorry, David," Tyler said. "There's no time to go back. You're shipping out this morning."

David thought he hadn't heard right.

"They need another internist at the 70th, and you could use the rest. If you hadn't fallen asleep last night, I'd have sent you out then. The chopper's coming at o-seven hundred." Tyler looked at his watch. "Better get your gear together. You have less than an hour."

David didn't know what to say, but he knew what he had to do.

"You don't understand," David said. "A few minutes is all I need. It'll be simple to look now. If I wait—I mean what happens if it starts raining, it'll be hopeless.

"David," Tyler said, "it's not going to rain for a while, and this is only going to be for a couple of days."

"A couple of days!"

"We all know how you feel, David. I saw him, too. But you'll be back before the end of the week. If you want to go out then and look . . . okay. But believe me, you don't have to. No one but us will ever know what happened to him."

David left Tyler standing in the doorway and walked to the motor pool. As he turned the corner of the head-quarters building, he saw that the gate to the motor pool was closed. He didn't have to walk over. He knew it would be locked. A sense of desperation gripped him. He had to go back. If he didn't, it would never really be over. It might be enough to try, but he wasn't even able to do that. Part of both of them would always be there now. There would be no way to forget. For someone who thought he was smart, he'd been real dumb.

David broke down the launcher and put it in his duffel bag, tucking it in under his clothes along with the grenades and shotgun rounds. He put the Sted-man's on top of his clothes and, leaving the duffel in the barracks, went to the freezer in the rear of the supply building.

He opened the large steel door and stepped inside. The door closed automatically behind him. A single unshielded bulb lit the frosted shelves. David walked down the aisle. They had put the body in the back on the bottom shelf. The cold began to stiffen his fingers.

He had come to say good-bye, but in the cold, he realized there were to be no farewells. What you needed to say your good-bye was time, and that was gone. How blind he'd been. They had been all alone, only the two of them out in the middle of nowhere, a fake radio, pretending nothing could happen.

Tom would have had a better chance, David thought, if he'd stayed in the Delta. There'd have been plasma there, medics, a real radio. They both would have had a better chance.

There was a tag attached to the body bag. David, with an aimless gesture, turned it over. Printed on the surface in block letters were the words REMAINS NON-VIEWABLE. So that was what Tyler had meant about no one else knowing. David continued to stare at the tag. How many of these were printed, he wondered; ten thousand, fifty thousand, a million? At least someone knew enough to think ahead. He let the tag drop and looked at the body.

"We should have burned the tires," he said. "You could have seen the smoke out on the flats for miles. Someone would have come. I could have stayed then. But you knew that, didn't you . . ."

David stayed with Tom until the cold drove him out.

Tyler was out at the helipad. "Got all your gear?" he yelled over the noise of the chopper.

"All I need, anyway."

"I hope you won't mind," Tyler said as he moved closer, cupping his hands over his mouth so David could hear, "but I wrote Tom's parents last night . . ."

David nodded.

"Well, take care . . . see you in a few days."

The crew chief in the doorway took David's duffel and then, reaching down, helped him climb on board. The sound of the engine rose in pitch.

The chopper lifted off the pad and rotated slowly about its axis. In a single moment all of the 40th swung past. David remembered his first impression, that it wasn't much of a base. Then, with a surge of power, the chopper lifted off the pad. Within minutes they were out over the plateau.

The door gunner pulled the machine gun away from its wall mounting, pointed it out the hatchway and cleared the chamber with two short bursts.

David sat back on the seat and watched the flats pass under them as he thought about everything that had happened. From that height the plateau, with its muted mixture of browns and greens, looked tranquil, almost innocent, and yet this land had tried to kill him twice, and had murdered . . . My God, David thought, leaning his head wearily against one of the door struts, had it only been four months?

David felt a tapping on his shoulder. The crew chief leaned close and pointed down toward a tree line. The trees had been burned. In the middle of the grove were the charred remains of three tanks. "Russian tanks!" he yelled over the din of the engine, and then, leaning forward, gave David a quizzical look. David turned and looked in the direction of the 40th and kept looking for a long time.

The 70th

Chapter 31

The chopper landed at the 70th, and for David it was as if he had been transported into another world. Boots were shined. Fatigue sleeves were all rolled to the regulation three inches above the elbow and everyone saluted everyone else.

In utter amazement he walked past the huge commissaries, down streets lined with bowling alleys and penny arcades. He stopped and looked into barber shops and pizza parlors where civilians and soldiers alike laughed and joked. Air Force and Army colonels and generals were everywhere. They walked around together like businessmen at a convention. There were billboards and advertisements tacked to lampposts. David stopped and with a mixture of bitterness and amusement read a sign in front of one of the beer halls announcing the arrival for a one-week engagement at the 70th of the Blue Bells, a country-and-western singing group "straight from Alabama." There seemed to be almost as many women as men at the 70th: nurses, WACs, stewardesses from the commercial planes using the base, and USO tours. He stood in the center of one of the side streets and gawked at two blondes who walked past in nothing but shorts and halter tops.

Everywhere there was a sense of confidence. The air was filled with the roar of fighter bombers as they took off from the Air Force base that occupied the whole northern end of the 70th. The hospital was next to the main airstrip, separated from the rest of the 70th by the motor pool. Twice a day, on his way to and from the hospital, David would walk past the acres of trucks and armored personnel carriers, the hundreds of tanks and self-propelled weapons. The 70th was not only the personnel center for central Vietnam but the supply depot for all of II Corps.

Whoever had cut his orders at the 40th had made them so vague that no one at the hospital knew what to do with him except assign him to the general medical clinics. The truth was that his orders had been written virtually to guarantee him a holiday. He could have done as he pleased, losing himself at the officers' club, in the beer halls, at the movies, swimming, loafing around in the bachelor officers' billet or finding a woman. But he didn't want to do any of those things, so to the surprise of the hospital adjutant and his new colleagues in the dispensary, he took his assignment seriously and showed up each day for the clinics and even agreed to take night call.

The doctors were all pleasant enough. At first there had been questions about his cut face and taped ribs, which David dismissed by saying he'd had an accident. And a few of the physicians his own age had asked about what it was like to be out in the boonies. But neither issue was ever pursued. Inevitably the talk

would turn to home, the next R and R, or the stewardesses and nurses at the 70th.

The majority of doctors saw their time at the 70th as
a job. David didn't blame them. The hospital was huge,
with everything from arterial bypass grafts to retinal
surgery being performed. It was the largest evac hospital in Nam, and its size and complexity, like that of
the base itself, made the war seem very far away. The
patients who arrived at the helipad were taken immediately into triage, where they were evaluated, and
from there into the stabilization room or surgery. It was
like any major trauma center in the States, and, indeed,
the physicians acted as if they were dealing with patients pulled in off some nearby freeway or intersection
down the block.

But at night, David noticed, things changed. As soon
as it started to get dark, heavily armed gunships took
off from the airfield and began to patrol the perimeter
of the base. Star shells, too, would be fired at fifteen-
minute intervals, lighting the sky with a metallic glow
so unearthly that no one acted or talked as confidently
as during the day. It was then that some of the physicians sitting around in the clinic or on the wards would
voice their concerns about the possibility of being
transferred out of the 70th. David listened, wondering
if their optimism and cheerfulness during the day were
nothing more than a strategy to keep from being la-
beled as malcontents and running the risk of reassign-
ment.

The main hospital buildings lay right up against the
northeast perimeter of the base. Each time David arrived, he would stop at the hospital gate and look out

over the fence and coils of razor wire past the rows of claymores to the patchwork of paddies and hedgerows a quarter-mile beyond the perimeter. The second day, walking back to the hospital with one of the surgeons, he paused.

"You know," David said, looking at the wire, "putting the hospital out here wasn't so smart." He pointed to the tree line. "If an attack comes from out there, there's nothing to stop 'em. They could use the broken ground from that tree line to get through the claymores. At night with all the shadows, there'd be enough cover, star shells or not, to get right to the fence, and then a few snips with a wirecutter and they're into the hospital. Be hard to contain them in here, and once in the hospital compound it's a short run to the choppers and flight line."

"Oh," the surgeon said, mistaking David's comments for worry. "I wouldn't be concerned. They might as well try to hit Saigon as the 70th."

"But in Saigon," David said dryly, "they wouldn't have to move patients." He nodded toward the orthopedic ward, the back door only a dozen meters from the fence. "There'll be no time to get out the patients in traction. They'll be killed in their beds."

"That's a little morbid, isn't it?"

David, incredulous, stared at the surgeon. "For who?" he asked. "You or the kids pinned to their beds?"

On his fourth day, a little after noon, he was leaving through the back door of the dispensary when he saw, a quarter-mile past the wire, a group of Vietnamese traveling cross-country. He couldn't see them clearly, but he was sure they were all men.

He sat on the back steps and waited. Half an hour later he saw what he was looking for—another group out beyond the tree line. He didn't go to lunch. An hour later a third group appeared along the horizon.

There were dozens of aircraft and choppers taking off and coming into the 70th every hour. Someone had to have seen the Vietnamese, maybe even have checked them out. He was not going to waste his time explaining to anyone, but he wasn't going to ignore it either. He didn't intend to make the same mistake twice.

Whatever happened, it wouldn't be during the day. Dawn or dusk, that was what Tom had said and that was when it would be.

In the evening David waited until he was alone in the barracks, went to his locker and took out his duffel. Sitting on his bed, he removed the Stedman's, unpacked the launcher and assembled the parts. He loaded it with a grenade and taped a shotgun and second grenade round to the stock, and then he sat there, staring at the dictionary. Finally he picked it up and, holding it gently for a moment, being sure not to loosen the paper markers, put it back in the duffel. He quickly wrapped the launcher in a towel and, leaving the barracks, went back to the hospital, where he hid it under the steps of the dispensary building. Any attack would take time to reach the barracks. He'd be able to get away from there. The hospital was the dangerous place.

In the end it was the silence that saved him. He was taking night call and was in the surgical wing of the dispensary building helping one of the surgeons sew up a trooper who'd cut his leg in a fall when he held up his hand, stopping the surgeon from putting in the next suture, motioning everyone to stay quiet.

David walked softly to the window, which had been left open to let in the cooler evening air. The crickets had stopped chirping. There wasn't a sound. No one in the room moved. It was as if they, too, had suddenly sensed the danger. A moment later he heard a faint metallic click.

"Get down!" he yelled and started running for the door as the side wall of the clinic blew. The blast hurled him forward. A second explosion caved in the back wall, sending splinters of wood and steel ricocheting down the length of the ward. The force of the second blast threw David through the screen door. Outside, bluish-green tracers skipped and skidded through the morning darkness.

As he scrambled to his feet, a series of explosions like tiny flares went off, lighting up the perimeter. With the explosions, the noise of the automatic fire rose in intensity, the tracer rounds growing so thick they caused the mist to glow. A hundred yards away a great geyser of flame shot up into the air as the OR exploded. The flames lit the compound. All up and down the perimeter he could see figures moving in through the wire.

A rocket roared past. David threw himself down as it crashed into what was left of the clinic. The heat from the blast seared the back of his neck, and for a second or two he couldn't hear anything, but he could see that the firing had increased and was now coming from the whole perimeter. He crawled quickly back to the steps.

Dragging out the launcher, he moved away from what remained of the dispensary. There were more explosions. As the buildings behind the clinic burst into flames, people began to scream. David was preparing himself to move across the open space to the shelter of the ortho building when a mortar round exploded only a dozen yards away. He pressed himself flat waiting for the next round when a star shell exploded, lighting up the compound.

Everything came into instant relief as the compound and perimeter became flooded with the eerie silvered light. The shell started to drift downward as two half-naked troopers, one carrying a rifle, were caught in its glare. David lay motionless as the troopers hurried to the corner of the ortho building for cover. Another mortar round hit near the building. Both the troopers stopped, silhouetted against the wall.

As he began to crawl forward, a string of tracers ripped through the air so close that he pressed himself flat again. When he looked up, the corner of the orthopedic ward and the two troopers were gone. There were new screams from inside the building. David looked behind himself to his right. In the fading glow of the star shell, three figures, no more than thirty meters away, crouching as they moved forward, stepped out of the smoke and mist. Another rocket shot overhead, but David kept his eyes on the men. The three figures kept moving closer, picking their way carefully across the cluttered ground.

Still watching, David started to move. As soon as he did, one of the figures suddenly dropped to one knee and shrugged a satchel charge from his shoulder. The figure next to him stood still. David froze. A round hit the ground a few feet in front of him. He fought the impulse to get up and run. He knew as surely as he'd ever known anything that one of them had seen him move. The certainty that they'd kill him the moment he moved again and the knowledge of what he had to do were strangely calming. He had the edge. The flames and shadows had confused them. They weren't sure. Tom's warning came back to him. "You've got to stop everything and get them first."

David slowly shifted his weight and at the same time swung the launcher around. He pulled the trigger as a second round buried itself in the dust directly ahead of him. The grenade bounced once as it hit the ground. The figures hesitated. David could almost feel their confusion, but it was too late. The grenade went off, killing all three even as they tried to jump away. David rolled to his left and quickly cracked open the barrel. As he tore the shotgun round loose from the stock, an artillery round landed seventy yards from him on the open ground just inside the wire. The concussion from the blast stunned him. A second round hit closer.

David quickly got to his feet as the air around him filled with the roar of a dozen speeding freight trains. The ground began exploding around him. The launcher was torn from his hand. He stumbled backward, but there was no place left to go. The breath was sucked from his lungs. Gasping, he spun around, losing consciousness as the earth rose toward him.

Zama

Chapter 32

"The object," Major Mitchell said, "is not to hurt yourself. Second operations take longer to heal than first ones. Patients are always sicker the second time. Nutrition's poorer because of the first operation; muscle tone's minimal, if it's there at all; and there's all that newly formed scar tissue, always weaker than normal connective tissue."

David continued to dress. The major, since he'd discovered David was a doctor, had deluged him with theories about everything from the best foods to eat before a marathon to how much pain different ethnic groups can tolerate. David wasn't sure about the major's other opinions, but there was no doubt he was right at least about second operations being worse than first ones. It was not so much the pain as the prolonged weariness. He had lain in bed for days after the second operation, barely able to move. It was an effort to lift his head, to reach for a glass. There was no energy left. Sleep made no difference, nor did the IV fluids or even food. It was as if his heart, brain and lungs were all functioning, but with no real connection to each other or to any other part of his body.

For days he was alive, but that was about all. David never would have thought it, but there were times when the pain following the first operation seemed preferable to the profound exhaustion after the second. Indeed, the pain was really all that David remembered of the first. Even three weeks later only bits and pieces of what had occurred after the bombardment had come back to him.

He remembered lying on the ground being unable to breathe, the terrible sense of suffocating. There were people running past. He could hear voices. He knew he was outside in the air; yet he was drowning. In a few seconds he'd be dead. Someone kneeled beside him. Then suddenly there was a pain in his side and as if by a miracle he could breathe again.

Someone was shouting for a medic. But there was another voice closer, telling him to hold still, that everything would be okay. David didn't believe it. He tried to move, but something was holding him down. "Hey," the voice said, "your lungs collapsed; there's a drain in your side; don't move." Someone lifted him. David fainted with the pain. When he did open his eyes again, he was staring up into a bank of fluorescent bulbs swinging back and forth above his head.

A surgeon, still in a scrub suit, had somehow materialized out of the surrounding darkness and was standing beside him. David remembered the greens were splattered with blood and so soaked with sweat that the cloth stuck to the doctor's body. The surgeon was talking to him. "If I had my way, I'd keep you here a few more days until the drains and tubes come out, but everyone who can make it is being evaced to Japan.

I've written the morphine orders for the flight. Sorry," he said, "but we need the beds."

An hour later David was on an ambulance bus. For some reason he remembered the ride clearly. They had passed one destroyed building after another, and those still standing were pockmarked with rocket and bullet holes.

At the gate to the air base, hollow-eyed troopers covered with dirt sat on top of their armored personnel carriers, nervously fingering the triggers of their M-60s.

From the bus as far as he could see, the field was a cemetery of charred wreckage. The main terminal building was a burned-out shell. There was nothing left of the dozens of flight lines. Parked helicopters and planes had been destroyed where they sat. In places the concrete had been scorched black by the heat of the burning metal. The ambulance bus maneuvered past the wrecks out onto the tarmac. At the far end of the field half a dozen C-141s were clustered protectively well away from the broken fences.

Grim-faced Air Force corpsmen off-loaded the patients two at a time. No one spoke. As the wounded were carried to the planes, the flight nurses stopped each litter to check the tags and medication orders. David got his second morphine injection. But as soon as the engines started up, the vibrations began to work their way through the bandages into his wounds, rubbing the nerve endings together. He clenched his teeth to keep from crying out. It was as if his wounds were on fire. By the time the plane was ready to take off, he was soaked with perspiration. He fainted for the first time less than a minute after takeoff. When he started to vomit, they took his litter forward and started an IV.

He was told that the trip from Vietnam to Japan was less than five hours, but it seemed more like days. Every other pain he'd known in his life had gradually gone away. His stomachaches had subsided; the pulled muscle in his thigh had gotten better; his broken leg had mended; even the headache from his encephalitis had eventually disappeared. All he'd ever had to do before was wait and it would be over, or at least not get any worse. But this was different. He tried to shift, take the weight off first his right side and then his left. He bent his legs under him to help lift his chest off the litter, took small breaths. But nothing worked; the pain only increased. He was given more morphine, but soon that, too, was of no use.

Each minute of the flight tore away another layer of his life. Conviction and confidence vanished, then any remaining sense of order and finally control. There was no one to help. He was utterly alone. Soon even that didn't matter anymore. In a world that should have held possibility, he was left shivering, incoherent.

David awakened to a rush of cool, wet air. The vibrations had stopped. The back of the plane was open, and through the bay of the cargo area he found himself staring, dazed, at a steel-gray sky. It took him a moment to realize it was raining. It was still raining when, two hours after landing at Zama, the main U.S. Army Hospital in Japan, they wheeled him into surgery.

What they had not had time to do in the makeshift OR at the 70th was done by the surgeons in Japan. They removed two infected ribs and a lobe of his right lung. They operated on his abdomen, resecting a quarter of his liver and removing two pieces of shrapnel, one lodged near his aorta and the other near the right kidney. The operation took eight hours. He had received fourteen units of whole blood and five units of fresh plasma before they were done.

It took David days to understand the true seriousness of the military disaster, but even in the recovery room he began to have a sense of the dimensions of what had happened. Troopers were being wheeled in from units across all of Vietnam. Isolated support and fire bases, province capitals, even large cities had been hit.

The story was much the same as at the 70th. Bases had been hit at dawn, the communists through the wire before anyone knew it. Many of the smaller units were overrun in the first hour. The larger bases had had time to react, containing the initial attacks, though the casualties were staggering. It was when they started to wheel in troopers who had been stationed in Saigon itself that David knew there had been a reckoning of gigantic proportions. When after a few days they started to push beds together to make room for more patients, he was sure of it.

David found things even worse once they transferred him out of recovery. The hospital was running out of space. The surgical wards had beds in the aisles. There were three chopper runs a day from the Air Force base at Yokota to the four U.S. Army hospitals near Tokyo. So many patients were being evaced in that as soon as one new group of patients had been processed, the next were already being rolled off the helipad. David counted fifty evacs in one afternoon run alone, and there were three other hospitals.

He listened to cooks and clerk typists tell of having

to grab rifles and fight to keep their units from being overrun. He listened while riflemen spoke in hushed tones, as if they were embarrassed that someone from the hospital might hear, of hanging on till morning expecting daylight to bring the gunships and fighter bombers, only to have to fight on through the rest of the day and the next night. Troopers talked of killing NVA and VC at distances of three and four feet, of using the bodies of friends as sandbags to keep themselves alive another hour. They spoke of falling asleep in the middle of firefights and waking up to find everyone around them dead. David heard the same stories told and retold a dozen times, always with the same sense of bewilderment. "Hell," one kid said, "it was like World War One."

Major Mitchell was talking to David. "Tomorrow, same time." He handed David's chart to the corpsman standing beside him. "And no more running; I mean it. You haven't healed yet; you could hurt yourself." But David was distracted. He was watching a trooper three tables down. He had been watching him ever since the major had started to talk.

The trooper, a lean blond kid, had limped in on crutches while the major was looking at David's suture line. He'd gone right to one of the exercise tables. There were curtains around the treatment tables, but he didn't close them.

He'd leaned his crutches against the wall and, sitting down, ignoring all the comings and goings around him, stretched out his leg so that the top of his foot hooked under the padded extensor arm at the end of the table.

A huge surgical scar ran from the upper part of his thigh down across what was left of his knee joint to his ankle. From where he sat, David could see that not only was his knee gone but a good part of the muscles of his leg too. The trooper grabbed the sides of the table and clenched his teeth as he struggled to straighten his leg. Beads of sweat broke out on his forehead, but the leg wouldn't extend. He tried again and again, but nothing happened.

"Did you hear me?" the major said.

David, still watching the trooper, didn't answer. Whatever else this kid wanted to do, David thought, he'd have to learn to do it without that leg. "Sure," David finally answered.

"All right," Mitchell said, "tomorrow, same time; and no more running."

Chapter 33

David turned down a side hallway marked TO LOWER COMPLEX. The corridors were empty. The morning evacs had all been processed and were either in surgery or on the wards. Here and there pushed up against the wall was a stretcher or wheelchair left by some enterprising orderly. Army regulations were to have the corridors clear at all times. A few more days of all these evacs, David thought, and it would be more than a matter of ignoring regulations; the machinery of the hospital itself would start breaking down. One of the service corps officers had told him that the OR had gone to three shifts and that even with that they were falling behind and thinking of opening a second operating area down in one of the empty buildings of the lower complex. The labs were all working overtime, and most of the corpsmen and specialists were already on twelve-hour duty rosters.

Tet, as the offensive was unofficially called, had caught everyone from battalion commanders to the generals at MACV by surprise. Worse, it had caught them unprepared. A captain evaced from Saigon who

ended up in a bed on David's ward told him that the
first reports indicated that the NVA and VC had infil-
trated between forty and sixty thousand troops in the
months before Tet and then concentrated these forces
in and around fifty to a hundred U.S. bases, most province capitals, and the major cities of Hue and Saigon
in the weeks before the offensive. They'd hit them all
the same morning and, according to the report, most at
precisely the same hour.

"No one believed what was happening for the first
twelve hours. Hell," he said, "there was so much going
on we didn't know where to send reinforcements first.
They even hit the embassy in Saigon. I'll tell you," he
went on, "someone's going to have to explain all this.
You can't have the enemy infiltrate all those troops
across a supposedly occupied country and then let
them set up for a nationwide offensive without anyone
knowing it, and not have people wanting to know why
and how."

Yet from what David could tell, the hospital personnel did not share the captain's view. They were worried
by the numbers of casualties and genuinely concerned
about the patients, trying their best to handle the increase in evacs, but strangely indifferent to the cause
of it all. It was as if they were just workers on some
production line where the conveyor belts had speeded
up, with everyone having to work faster and faster to
keep up, willing to push themselves to exhaustion
rather than ask what was happening or, more important, if something might have gone wrong with the
machinery itself. It seemed incredible until David realized that like the doctors at the 70th, they didn't want

to know. It was as if it were better for them to believe that someone was in charge than to ask questions and perhaps find out the truth or, by asking, label themselves as troublemakers. Still, he noticed that the pressure of more and more wounded was having its own effect.

Even Mitchell, so confident at first, had gradually lost some of his pompousness as he scrambled to readjust schedules to accommodate the rising number of incoming wounded. The corpsmen and enlisted personnel, too, over the weeks since the offensive had become quieter, less talkative. They weren't fools, and they could tell that with all the wounded there would have to be some reassignments to Vietnam. The U.S. bases in Japan were the ones closest to Southeast Asia.

David walked out the rear door of the hospital and started down the grassy slope toward the lower complex. The hospital was built in a great semicircle, the two end wings overlooking the lower complex, a group of buildings set out in the middle of what was left of an old polo field. The main hospital as well as the polo field had been built in the 1930s by the Japanese as part of their military academy. The Americans had taken over the base at the end of the second world war and during the Korean War had added the buildings of the lower complex as a support area for the hospital. Part of the complex had already been reopened with the increase in casualties and was being used as an outpatient department and blood bank. Construction crews had remodeled one of the buildings into a surgical ward and were in the process of turning another into an operating and recovery suite.

As he walked down the slope, David saw someone standing in the corner window at the end of the east wing. It was the psychiatric area, and David noticed with some surprise that whoever it was wore a mustache. It was the first mustache he'd seen in the Army.

David crossed the street that separated the hospital from the lower complex and headed across the open field toward the half-dozen concrete buildings. But he didn't stop at the buildings. As he had done for over a week, he walked past them toward an old wooden utility shack that sat beside a section of abandoned road, marking the furthest edge of the hospital property.

Chapter 34

David stepped off ten more yards on the road than he had the day before. He hadn't planned on running, but when after two weeks of physical therapy he still felt weak, he had decided something else had to be done. His muscle tone was returning, but he had no sense of strength or endurance. There was no reserve, nothing to draw on.

Mitchell had told him not to worry, that strength would come with time, but David had no intention of waiting. He would never wait for anything again. As for the major's pronouncement, he'd had enough of experts. No one would ever tell him what he should or shouldn't do again. Any belief David had had in expertise had died for good when the first mortar round blew in the rear wall of the dispensary.

David began getting back into shape by walking around the hospital grounds, at first once and then twice a day, trying each time to cut a minute or two off the time of the preceding circuit. It was on one of his walks that he saw the utility shack and next to it found the road, a hundred yards of forgotten, weed-covered cinder that started nowhere and ended nowhere.

The first day David made it a little over ten yards. It wasn't much of a run; he couldn't even call it jogging. It was more just hobbling along, but at least he was moving again.

Mitchell had been outraged. "You tore the suture line!"

"I pulled it," David corrected.

"Pulled it? Look here at the corner."

David had been surprised to see that there was a little blood. The major was furious.

"You're not helping one bit," he said.

"It doesn't hurt," David said as he continued to dress.

"Scar tissue doesn't hurt till it tears."

"Really?" David asked. "That true all the time?"

Mitchell flushed, and David left it at that.

It took David four more days to make it half the length of the road. It was toward the end of his third week in Japan that he ran his first hundred yards.

Afterward he had to sit on what was left of the steps of the shack and wait over half an hour till he could straighten up again, but it was worth it. The running was getting him back into shape in a way that Mitchell's isometrics never could. The minimum you had to do was be able to move.

Reluctantly, as he sat there, David found himself thinking of the 40th. He had looked for someone from the 40th ever since he'd left the recovery and was sent to the ward. There were three other military hospitals in Japan and another, he'd been told, in Okinawa. They could have been evaced there. There was a chance, too, that the 40th had been spared, though David wasn't so sure about that. The communists wouldn't have left the

40th sitting in their rear. Some might have made it, though. Thorpe would have known what to do. If they had survived the initial assault, a few could have hung on. What had Tyler said to him? That he could see in the dark? It wasn't much, but in the morning shadows, it might have been enough. A little edge was sometimes all you needed. After all, he was alive.

David tried again and made it another twenty yards. He was able to stand up again just as the choppers bringing in the afternoon med evacs began to land. The new litter patients were in the corridors when he walked back into the hospital. He looked carefully at each of the faces of the wounded as he passed.

He was walking down the main corridor past the clinics when he heard a commotion coming from the hallway leading down to the outpatient department. David stopped. A moment later the double doors of the surgical clinic flew open and a corpsman came running out.

Through the open doors David could hear the sound of furniture being moved. The corpsman ran past him. People were yelling. Someone was calling for a tourniquet. David glanced back toward the main corridor. He saw doctors and hospital personnel walking by, but no one turned down the hallway. There was more noise coming from the clinic. Damn, David thought, I'm done with this. He looked back. No one was coming.

David didn't remember moving. One moment he was standing there waiting for someone to come and the next he was pushing his way into the clinic through the crowd blocking the center aisle. A patient, the bottoms of his hospital pajamas soaked with blood, lay sprawled on the floor. The tables and chairs had been shoved aside to give him room.

David kneeled beside the trooper, pressing his hand over the darkest part of the stain. The trooper, startled, looked up at him, his eyes wide with fright. David felt the bulge and pressed down harder.

"Don't move," David said. "It's okay. I'm a doctor. You," David said, picking out the nearest patient, "get his chart! And you," he said, seeing another corpsman, "call the blood bank and tell them we're going to need twelve units of blood." David picked up the trooper's dog tags with his free hand. "A positive," he said.

"My leg started to bleed," the trooper said. "All I did was stand up and start walking. All of a sudden my pants was covered with blood."

"It's all right," David said. "Just relax."

"They said I was okay. I mean," the trooper said, his voice edgy with panic, "I mean they said everything was fine, nothing to worry about."

The patient returned with the chart.

"Read the cover page." David felt the bulge shift under his palm and pressed down harder. The trooper stiffened. "Don't move," David warned. "It's all right; just don't move."

" 'Gunshot wound,' " the patient read, " 'ruptured iliac artery, ilial-femoral bypass graft.' "

"How long ago was the operation?"

The patient searched for the entry. " 'Graft placed February tenth, 90th evac,' " he said.

David turned back to the trooper. He was staring at David, the look of fear etched on his face. Startled, David saw the panic right below the surface. It seemed to hold him. For a moment David forgot where he was as visions of waves of heat rising off the flats swept over him.

"Look," David said quickly, fighting off the dizziness that came with his own confusion, "they just put in an arterial graft at the 90th to replace your own artery. The graft is leaking a bit, that's all. It happens sometimes. You had any fever in the last few days?"

"Yeah," the trooper said, "but they said not to worry. They told me it was a cold or flu." He looked frightened again. "Why?"

"Sometimes grafts get infected. I think they're going to have to reoperate, take a look and maybe put in a new one."

David, his arm weakening, shifted his position to get more of his own weight over the mass.

"Relax," he said. "There's still a lot of pressure. Means that you haven't lost too much blood."

"What's going on here?" A captain wearing one of the long white lab coats that the clinic doctors wore stepped up beside the two of them.

"This fellow's femoral graft is leaking a little," David said, surprised at the calmness of his own voice. It was as if someone else were speaking for him.

"He's a doctor," one of the patients whispered.

"Better get the surgeons." David turned back to the trooper. "They do this kind of repair all the time around here. Captain," David said, "I'd get the stretcher." It was not a request but a demand. "Now!" he said angrily. The captain, startled, left.

"You're gonna stay . . . right?" the soldier said.

"Sure."

The trooper lowered his voice so that only David could hear. "Doc," he whispered, "do you really think they can get me out of this?"

David hesitated. "You've got a chance." The trooper's lips tightened, but he didn't ask anything else.

The captain, accompanied by two medics, brought in the stretcher and put it down beside the trooper. The trooper took hold of David's other hand; then, when David nodded, the medics lifted the trooper and slipped the stretcher under him.

As David moved, a sharp pain shot through his side. He managed to stifle his gasp. The trooper stiffened.

"You okay?" he whispered nervously.

"Yeah," David answered, "I'm okay."

It took only two minutes to get to the OR, but by the time they got there David could no longer feel his right side.

The operating room was ready, the doors leading to the surgical suite held open. They carried the stretcher through the open doors directly into the operating room. The surgeons, masked and gowned, were ready. As they put the stretcher down on the operating table, one of the surgeons stepped in behind David. Another moved up to the other side of the table. The trooper lifted his head and looked around and then, apparently satisfied, put his head back on the table. He looked at David. "Going to be around when I wake up?" he asked. Before David could answer, the anesthesiologist put a mask over the trooper's face.

The surgeon behind David moved closer. "When I say so, step to your right. Do it quickly, one motion. I'll move into your place."

There was a hiss of gas. A moment later the trooper's hand slipped free of David's.

"Blood pressure's dropping!"

A nurse stepped up to the table and pushed a large IV needle into a vein in the soldier's neck.

"The aneurysm's getting bigger," David said.

"Now," the surgeon ordered.

But as David started to move, the whole thigh began to swell. He pressed down again. Another pain shot through his side. This time he gasped, but he didn't let go.

"Heart rate's one eighty. Pressure's sixty over zero!"

The surgeon pushed David aside. As his hand came off the thigh, a great geyser of blood and muscle shot into the air. There was a great deal of hectic movement about the table as a familiar smell suddenly engulfed the room. It was the odor of rotting fruit.

Stunned, David stepped back from the table. It took him a few moments to collect himself. During those seconds the OR had quieted, falling into its usual, more ordered routine.

David watched as the surgeons worked and the corpsmen and nurses walked back and forth, setting up new trays, carrying in new equipment. As he stood there, ignored, surrounded by the clinking of instruments and the hiss of the ventilator, his attention was drawn to the suction bottles slowly filling with blood. The bottles were fastened to a wall socket a few feet from the operating table. Two sets of tubing ran from the table to the bottles. He watched as inch by inch the level rose. They hung more units of blood. The surgeon at the head of the table mumbled something and a nurse left the table, walked to the wall suction and turned the valve. The blood siphoned off from the first container, splashed into a second bottle, and then slowly, as with the first, began to rise. They hung more units of blood but the more they hung the faster the bottle filled.

David knew, as the blood continued to rise, that they would never be able to stop the bleeding. When he'd lifted his hand, whatever had been left of the infected graft had torn loose. Even in a hospital, with operating rooms only minutes away, with all the blood and plasma you could need, surrounded by all the latest gear, there was no difference. There was no way to clamp an artery that wasn't there anymore. You were killed in Nam, but you could die anywhere. The only way to survive was never to have become part of it. What had Plunkett told him the day the chopper crashed? "They all burn." He should have listened. David watched the bottles that would not stop filling with blood. And he didn't even know the trooper's name. The idea that he had chosen all this to ensure a career that hadn't even started left him almost as bewildered as it did angry.

David left the OR, and as he stepped back into the main corridor he realized he couldn't feel his right side. But he didn't care.

He looked up at the clock over the mess hall entrance. It was time for physical therapy.

David took the first unoccupied treatment table. He didn't see Mitchell come up behind him.

"You're bleeding!"

"Bleeding?" David said, looking down at the front of

his shirt, seeing the bloodstains from the OR. "It's not mine."

Mitchell pointed toward his side. "I don't mean the front," he said angrily.

David lifted his arm. A red streak ran from his armpit to the bottom of the shirt.

"I've warned you about all that running. Now let me see it. Let's go," Mitchell said, annoyed. "Take off your shirt. I don't have all day. In case you haven't noticed, we're trying to do something here."

"Do something!" David seemed to come out of himself.

"Let's go get it off. We don't have time to waste on patients who won't listen."

"What did you say?" Mitchell didn't hear the warning in David's voice. "Have you looked around, Major?" David said. "Go on, look!" The patients at the nearby tables had stopped their exercises. "What these kids need, Major, are arms and legs, not to learn how to drag themselves along on crutches or paint with their teeth."

"Corporal," Mitchell said to the corpsman, "I want this patient out of here."

"I'm not finished with my exercises," David warned.

The corpsman, suddenly wary, hesitated. David went back to the small barbell he'd set up.

"Corporal," Mitchell demanded, "I want this man out of here and on report."

"On report!" David was as amazed as he was amused.

What astonished him was that Mitchell actually believed that he'd listen. In the midst of all this, the major must have thought that nothing had changed, that despite everything it was still the same old game with all the old rules. It was that blindness that had led them all there in the first place.

"Stupid bastard," David mumbled, picking up a loose quarter-pound weight to balance the barbell.

"What did I hear you say?" Mitchell demanded. The major seemed to draw himself up even straighter than usual. "Jenkins, if this patient isn't out of here in three minutes, call the MPs."

David threw the weight. There was no time for Mitchell to react. His head jerked back and he stumbled sideways, his hands covering his nose and mouth. Twisting, he fell against one of the inclines. Getting up, blood running from between his fingers, he lurched down the center aisle and out the door.

There were a few moments of silence, and then, as if nothing had happened, everyone went back to his exercises. Fifteen minutes later David finished his workout and left the ward. He felt no malice toward the major, nor did he feel any remorse. If he felt anything, it was that he had done Mitchell a favor.

Chapter 35

The next morning after breakfast David went back to the lower complex. He was determined to continue with his program. He had torn his suture line, but only along the edges. He would have to be careful about stretching, but with the ribs and all the muscle gone, he'd have to watch out for that no matter what he did.

As for Mitchell, David did not give what had happened a second thought. He was convinced nothing would come of it. The Army was not about to publicize a fight between two officers. He understood that much about how the military worked. At least, he thought with little satisfaction, he'd learned something in the last few months.

David had planned to run the whole distance but he made it less than half what he'd done the day before. He was tired. His energy was gone. He decided to try it again, determined to fight the growing sense of exhaustion. He was resting, waiting to catch his breath, retying his shoelaces before he began a second time, when he saw a lone officer walk down the slope from the main hospital. There was a constant traffic of pa-

tients and hospital personnel between the two com-
plexes, but there was something familiar about this
officer.

"Shit," David said as the colonel changed direction
and started to walk directly toward him.

"Congratulations," the colonel said. He was wearing
a mustache. "I never thought you'd make it even part
of the way." David saw the medical insignia on the
colonel's collar. "My office is up there," the colonel
said, gesturing up the slope in the general direction of
the hospital. "It overlooks the lower complex. As I remember, you ran almost the whole length of the road
yesterday, a great improvement from your first try.
But," he added pleasantly, "you're obviously a determined fellow. My name's Ed Rollins." The colonel was
a big man, overweight, but despite his size his uniform
fit neatly, giving him the well-kept look of the career
Army officer. David stared at the mustache.

"I know, they fell out of favor right after Custer," the
colonel answered as if David's look were a question.

"Custer, huh," David said dryly, going back to tying
his shoes.

"Not a popular name these days, but take my word
for it, mustaches will come back." He smiled. "There's
a rhythm to these things." But he added quickly, "I
didn't think Major Mitchell had hundred-yard dashes
as part of his physical therapy program."

"They're hardly dashes." David looked again at the
colonel. "I've seen you somewhere before. You were at
the window of the . . ." He hesitated.

"Psychiatric wing. I'm a psychiatrist. It's the reason
I'm allowed to wear the mustache. Generals think

we're able to read minds; so they leave us alone. It's never a good idea to cross the witch doctor."

David wasn't amused. He stood.

"Going back to the hospital?" the colonel asked. He didn't wait for an answer. "I'd like to walk along. I was thinking we might be able to help each other."

"Help each other?" David said, surprised.

"With what's going on, you don't think we could all use some help?"

"They sent you down to talk to me. A psychiatrist. Christ." David sighed. "That what they plan to do, Colonel? Tell us that what's happening is just in our minds?"

"No," the colonel answered matter-of-factly, "not likely. All right if I walk along?"

"Sure," David said. "Why not?"

They started toward the road.

"You were hit at the 70th, weren't you?"

David, suspicious, slowed down.

"I read your file," the colonel said. "Part of my assignment. I was sent here to write a report on the psychological effects of the offensive." He spoke calmly, without apology. "Part of that evaluation is to collect data from all the hospitals in Japan—numbers of evacs, types of operative procedures, any incidents, things like that; tedious but necessary." The colonel went on in the same conversational tone. "It appears as if our Major Mitchell has a blow-out fracture of his right orbit. He was operated on last night. I'm not a clinician, but there was something about double vision, muscles of the eye being detached. But," he went on, "you'd know more about that kind of thing than I would."

"Mitchell's a fool."

They reached the road and had to stop to let an ambulance pass.

"Maybe not a fool," the colonel offered. "A bit pompous and overbearing at times; boring, I'm sure; but competent at his work. A quality that, after all that's happened, shouldn't be lightly dismissed."

"He a friend of yours?"

"I haven't been here long enough to have friends," the colonel answered.

They started across the street together.

"Then they did send you about my fight with Mitchell."

"From what I heard it didn't last long enough to be called a fight. How about some coffee? I could use a cup and I assume your afternoon's free. I doubt," he added pleasantly, "you'd be welcome in physical therapy and I would like to talk to you."

David stopped. "About helping each other?"

"Yes."

"Sorry, I've seen military psychiatry in action," David said. "You don't need anyone's help. The Army's already got all the Thorazine it needs."

The colonel wasn't flustered. "And how would you handle combat fatigue?" he asked. "Like the Russians or the Chinese? Anyone leaves his position or refuses to go forward and it's desertion. No extenuating circumstances, no discussions. You have him shot right then and there, end of problem? Not very humane, but definitive, and I assume somewhat effective."

"So we give them drugs and send them back to their units; that's even more effective," David said. "They can still pull a trigger."

"You didn't answer the question," the colonel said.

He waited a moment. "The reality is, David, that we're here and we're fighting and no one knows exactly how to handle the stress of combat. Now that we've settled nothing," he went on, "how about that coffee? If you're worried about me, don't. I'm not Mitchell. I duck."

David laughed despite himself. "Sure," he said. "Why not?" They crossed the street together.

"I did read your file," Rollins said, "but like most, it wasn't very complete. Even in our Army there isn't much time for paperwork when units are being over-run. You were wounded at the 70th."

David nodded.

"I heard the hospital was hit pretty bad the first day, that they ended up doing surgery in one of the supply buildings."

"It didn't get hit the first day," David answered dryly. "It got hit the first minute. The attack on the 70th began at the hospital compound. They came through the hospital to get to the airfield. It was only a couple of hundred yards from the OR to the flight line. Blowing up the hospital was just a bonus."

The colonel gave David a quizzical look. "Well," he offered apologetically, "details get lost in memos."

"I'm sure they do." They continued to walk.

"There is something you should know, though," Rollins said. "It's one of the reasons I came down to find you. They plan to have you out of here by dinner."

David stopped walking.

"They're cutting the orders to get you home now. I know, it's a little quicker than usual," the colonel added gently, "but the generals don't want any more trouble."

But David wasn't listening anymore. He had known

he'd have to leave; he'd known it all along. No one stayed till the end. But still it came as a shock. Home. My God, David thought. The colonel might as well have told him he was going to the moon.

"Maybe we should talk about it," the colonel said.

"Talk about what?" David asked.

"Going home, the attack on the 70th." The colonel hesitated. "You were stationed at the 40th."

David nodded.

"They hit the plateau west of Saigon real hard." David said nothing. "You've been saved twice, haven't you?"

David, despite himself, turned pale. "But, of course," the colonel added, "you know that." The colonel waited. "It was a war, David," he said gently. "A lot of people didn't know that; or, like Mitchell, refuse to admit it."

The coffee shop was empty. Rollins led the way to a table near the back. "I'll get the coffee."

David sat down. He knew the colonel was right. They had to have hit the 40th. And he hadn't said good-bye to anyone. He'd just gone out to the helipad and left. Couple of days and he'd return. There would be no going back now. He'd left forever.

Going home wouldn't change anything. It surprised him that he'd been so startled to hear it. Home or not, it made no difference. He should have gone back to where he and Tom had been ambushed. The least you could do, remains viewable or not, was send all the pieces of your dead back to be buried.

The colonel put the cups on the table and sat down. He pushed the sugar bowl toward David.

"Tell me," David asked, strangely curious, "are the generals really wasting their time deciding what to do with me? I mean going to the trouble of having someone cut special orders to get me out when I'd be gone soon anyway?"

"They're worried," the colonel said. "Couple dozen enlisted men witnessed your attack on Mitchell. Three or four corpsmen, all the patients in PT at the time. The generals are concerned about morale."

"Morale," David said, amused. "You'd better tell them they have bigger problems than that."

Rollins reached across the table for the sugar. "They don't think so. Your attack on the major was the first act of violence between a patient and any of the hospital personnel. The generals are not as worried about losing the offensive as they are about losing an army. No matter how it may look now," the colonel continued, "the Tet offensive is going to end up a great military disaster for the communists. The most recent aerial reconnaissance shows that all the major bases have been retaken and that the bulk of communist troops in the countryside have all been isolated. It will only be a matter of time before they're killed or captured." He stirred sugar into his coffee. "The Army bent in a lot of places, but it never broke. It proved far better than even the Pentagon thought. Best estimates are two, three years for the communists to bring units in the south up to strength to take on the ARVNs, and three to five, if ever, to challenge the mainline U.S. forces."

"So it wasn't all for nothing. That's going to be the idea? I'd warn your generals to be careful," David said.

"Numbers can be deceiving over here. I do have to
hand it to the military, though. They're able to find
success in any catastrophe."

"And you?" Rollins asked.

"Me?" David said, surprised. "I've made it, Colonel."

"I don't think so," Rollins answered. "Running
hundred-yard dashes right after you've been severely
wounded and going after officers like Mitchell doesn't
sound to me like you've made it . . . Look, David," the
colonel said gently. "I think we can help each other.
When this is finally over, the Mitchells aren't even
going to be around anymore. There isn't going to be
anyone around that you know. There's not going to be
a single person for you or anyone else to blame except
yourself. I mean it about helping each other. There's
another assessment that can be made about Tet. I've
talked to a lot of troopers, and there's an almost univer-
sal feeling that for something as extensive as Tet to
have occurred, everyone in authority had to have
screwed up. The offensive, no matter what its military
outcome, will be a great psychological success for the
communists. We have enough military muscle to keep
the war going for a while. But the heart's out of it now
—whatever heart there was. It's a mess."

But David was looking past him, staring at the entrance. The colonel turned.

A number of corpsmen from the surgical clinic had
walked into the snack bar. One of the corpsmen left
the group and walked over to the table. "Excuse me,
sir," he said to David. "I don't know if you've been told,
but the patient you helped yesterday never made it out
of the OR."

"I know," David said. "Thanks."

"Yes, sir." The corpsman left.

Rollins waited.

"A casualty of your psychological defeat," David explained.

"Someone you knew?" the colonel asked.

"No, I doubt if anyone knew him." David pushed his chair away from the table. "Thanks for the coffee, Colonel."

"And Mitchell? What kind of casualty was he?"

"Casualty!" David snorted.

"What else would you call it?"

"A lesson," David answered coldly. "Believe me, Colonel, a fractured orbit's a small enough price to pay for learning to see what you're looking at."

"So you decided you'd teach him."

"Someone had to," David answered.

"Why?"

"He was pretending."

"Pretending?"

"That he could fix things."

"And of course he can't. Is that it?"

David didn't answer.

"This isn't a very sophisticated army, David. I doubt if there'll be any senators or presidents of big corporations coming from the enlisted ranks of these units. If people like you give up, there isn't going to be any hope for anyone."

"Hope!" David mimicked. "Sorry, Colonel," he said angrily, starting to leave. "You'll have to save that one for your report."

Suddenly he stopped, and stared at the colonel. "But

they're not going to read your report, are they?" David said. "No one's going to want to know about psychological defeats." He stared at the colonel as if seeing him for the first time. "Well"—David paused—"at least you're right about one thing: it *is* a mess."

"And with a little more time, it'll be a mystery."

"Maybe," David said.

"I can get you those extra days."

David smiled wearily. "Another day isn't going to change much."

"It can be a beginning. This isn't going to end when you get on the plane."

"Colonel," David answered, "it ended before either of us even got here."

ABOUT THE AUTHOR

Ronald J. Glasser graduated Phi Beta Kappa from Johns Hopkins University in 1961. He received his medical degree from Johns Hopkins Medical School in 1965. Dr. Glasser completed an internship and residency in the Department of Pediatrics of the University of Minnesota Medical School. He continued his medical education as a post-doctoral fellow of the National Institutes of Health in Pediatric Nephrology at Minnesota. Dr. Glasser is currently a pediatric nephrologist at the Park Nicollet Medical Center in Minneapolis and codirector of the Pediatric Rheumatology Clinic at the Gillette Hospital for Crippled Children in St. Paul. From 1968 to 1970, Dr. Glasser was a medical officer in the United States Army, stationed at the U.S. Army Vietnam Evacuation Hospital, Camp Zama, Japan, where he was cited for "meritorious service in keeping with the highest tradition of the United States Army." Dr. Glasser is the author of four books, including the widely acclaimed *365 Days*.